T0354491

BROKEN
HERO

BROKEN HERO

Power Tree

Xavier L Hernandez

BROKEN HERO
POWER TREE

iUniverse books may be ordered through booksellers or by contacting:

iUniverse
1663 Liberty Drive
Bloomington, IN 47403
www.iuniverse.com
1-800-Authors (1-800-288-4677)

ISBN: 978-1-5320-2374-3 (sc)
ISBN: 978-1-5320-2375-0 (e)

Library of Congress Control Number: 2017907144

Print information available on the last page.

iUniverse rev. date: 05/03/2017

For
Sky Griffin: Someone I'll never forget
To those who lost someone and need a hero

Part 1

Two glass doors slammed open as a boy threw them open. He ran over to a girl in a puddle of blood. He drops the hammer in his hand as he dropped to his knees next to the girl. The boy put both of his warm shaking hands on her blood-soaked shirt. The girl's eyes opened at his touch.

"I'm so cold," the girl said.

"I know you are cold." The boy said as his eyes started to water.

"Can you hold me Luis, please?" She said as a tear fell from her face.

"Of course," said Luis.

Luis moved his blood covered hands to lift the girl. He felt her cold skin against his warm body. He moved her black hair out of her face. Her brown eyes gazed into his eyes. Tears fell from his eyes. She moved a bloody hand to his face.

"Don't cry my love. I don't want to see tears come from your wonderful brown eyes. You have to make me an important promise or more." The girl said with a smile.

"What is it you ask of me," he asked.

"You have to keep those glasses clean and keep your black hair nice looking. Promise not to hurt Milena," the girl a said with a small groan.

"I can only promise you the first one. Milena is mad at me for leaving her to look for you," Luis said.

The girl started to laugh then groans in pain. Luis looked down to see her lips purple. Her eyes started to close. Luis shook her awake.

"Hey, you stay with me. Don't leave me," he said with tears streaming from his eyes.

"Promise you won't blame yourself for my death." She said as her eyes started to close again.

"I promise you my lovely sister," Luis whimpered.

"Goodbye my friend," she said.

"Desiree no, please don't go. You can't leave. You have family still here." Luis yelled in sadness.

"I love you but it's just my time to go," Desiree whispered.

Desiree's hand slipped from his face leaving a streak of blood on his face. More tears left Luis's eyes as he rocked back and forth with Desiree in his arms. Luis looked up at the ceiling and screamed. As he screamed the lights started to flicker until he stopped. Gunfire went off in the distance making him stop crying. He took the black leather jacket stained with blood off Desiree. Luis looked at the bullet holes in his jacket before he put it on. He moved Desiree's body from the puddle of blood to a clean spot on the shiny gold floor in the school gym. The sound of glass breaking outside in the hall put Luis into a sprint with the hammer in his hand.

"Please no, please don't kill us. We can help you." A man said in fear.

"Shut up," another man said in anger.

Students screamed as the security guard gets knocked into a trophy case. Luis gripped the hammer in his hand while he sneaked behind the tall man in a trench coat. The man aimed his shotgun at the security guard. Light flashed from the end as a loud crack filled the hallway. A short girl with blonde hair and green eyes saw Luis.

"You, white blonde girl come here," the man with the gun said.

"Make me bitch," the girl said.

The man aimed at the girl as Luis moved closer. A tall skinny pale boy jumped in front of the girl. Luis swung the hammer at the man's head. The man screamed and fired a shot. The girl crouched over the boy after he fell to the floor.

"You want to die boy," the gunmen asked.

"Prove you're a man by fighting me," Luis yelled.

"As you wish you filthy Mexican," the man yelled back.

Luis looked at the man as he dropped the shotgun. He looked into the green eyes behind the blood covered ghost mask. The man pulled two jagged knives from his belt. Luis got into a fighting stance with the sharp end of his hammer pointed at the man.

"You'll die at the hands of Ghost," Ghost said.

Luis waited for Ghost to swing twice at him before countering. Screams leave Ghost as the hammer went into his arm. Blood dripped onto the floor as the students watched in horror. Ghost kicked at Luis. Luis spun to the right while swinging the hammer. Ghost groaned as he felt pain in his side. Luis kicked the back of Ghost's knee. He fell to one knee while Luis slammed the hammer into Ghost's head. Blood squirted onto Luis's face as the hammer got ripped from Ghost's head. Luis dropped the hammer to the floor then moved to grab Ghost's arm.

"I have questions for you to answer," Luis said in a growl.

"Go to hell," Ghost said.

Luis broke Ghost's arm then watched the knife fall to the floor. Ghost screamed in pain as Luis grabbed the other arm.

"First question is easy. Where did you come from before the band room?" Luis yelled at Ghost.

"Your mother's house," Ghost said with a laugh.

Luis broke the arm then kicked Ghost's face. Ghost fell to the floor. Luis grabbed both knives. He lifted one of Ghost's leg then stabbed a knife through Ghost's foot. Screams left the students as Luis grabbed the other leg. Ghost laughed as he looked at Luis.

"How does it feel to torture someone? How does it feel to be on the edge of killing someone? The real question is can you live with yourself after killing someone." Ghost said with laughter in his voice.

"I can live with all these school shooter's blood on my hands," Luis responded.

"Then you are no better than us." Ghost said as he tried to move his arm.

"I'm better then you because I don't kill the innocent. Now where did you come from?" Luis said in anger.

"Your father's house," Ghost said with a smile.

Luis stabbed the knife into Ghost's foot. Ghost screamed then laughed. Luis picked up the hammer and climbed on top of Ghost.

"Who sent you to Cardinal High," Luis asked.

"Your brother, sister, and father," Ghost yelled.

"I don't have a father or siblings." Luis yelled as he raised the hammer.

Luis swung the hammer with all his strength. The girl watched as teeth and parts of the mask flew left and right.

Luis continued until the girl called said, "Luis stop he is dead."

The girl stood a few inches away from Luis. Luis looked down at Ghost's face. He realized that it on longer is something resembling a human face or skull. He continued to stare into the dark insides of Ghost's face. Bone, plastic, and skin swim in a pool of blood leaking from the back of Ghost's head. A student threw up at the sight of Ghost's once warm corpse. Luis looked out the glass door to see a golf cart under the dark cloudy sky. Luis walked over to the dead security guard and grabbed the keys off the man's belt.

"Luis is Desiree alright," the girl asked.

"No Milena," Luis responded.

"Where is she," Milena asked.

"In the gym dead. I'm getting you guys out of the school," Luis said.

"What about you?" Milena asked with a concerned look.

"I'm hunting the rest of these walking corpses and letting out whatever students I find as well," Luis said.

"Then I'm coming with you," Milena said.

"Not an option. I can fight them because I was trained by

my mother's boyfriend to fight. You can't come because you aren't trained to fight," Luis said angrily.

Milena stood quiet while Luis searched Ghost's body for the knife sheaths. After he found them and put them on his belt then he looked up at her.

"You better come back to me because I love you," Milena said.

"Is the boy who got shot alive," Luis asked.

"He just died. The gunshot took half of his face," she said sadly.

"Get the others to the gate next to the band room. I'll be behind you." Luis said with a tear in his eye.

Milena hugged Luis before getting the others up and ready to leave. Luis watched them leave then dragged Ghost's body to the golf cart. The cold air made Luis's hair dance. Luis put Ghost in the passenger's seat of the golf cart. He walked back into the red brick building with a sigh. Luis sheathed the knives and put the keys in his pocket. Luis picked up the shotgun then ran to the gate behind the band room.

"Luis behind you," Milena yelled.

Luis turned around to see a woman with two pistols in her hands. The students got to cover as she opened fire. Luis started running at the girl with a wolf mask to hide her face. He slid to the side as she swung at him. Luis turned and aimed at the girl. The girl screamed as Luis shot her left arm. The pistol in her left arm hit the floor while blood ran down her arm.

"How dare you strike Wolf," Someone yelled.

Luis ducked as a man with a skeleton mask covering his face swung his axe at Luis.

"Thank you for the help Skeleton," Wolf said in a gasp of pain.

"You are welcome Wolf," Skeleton replied.

Luis aimed at wolf and stood waiting for her to move. Skeleton moved forward making Luis squeeze off two shots. Wolf hit the floor dropping her pistol. Luis dodged a swing then hit Skeleton with the butt of the shotgun. Skeleton started to scream as part of his mask cracked.

"First you kill my women now you break my mask. Oh, how I'm going to enjoy killing you," Skeleton screamed.

Luis fired another round. The axe clattered to the floor as Skeleton's fingers flew into the air. He screamed in pain as Luis unsheathed the two knives. Skeleton threw a punch. Luis stabbed a knife into that hand then jabbed the other knife in his throat. Skeleton's mouth opened to spit out blood. Luis ripped the knife out by moving it to the left of his throat. Skeleton dropped to the floor as Luis sheathed one knife. Wolf moved her leg. Luis pulled the knife out of Skeleton's hand. As Luis walked over to Wolf he pulled the keys out of his pocket.

"Unlock the gate and leave the keys," Luis called to Milena.

Luis threw the keys to Milena. She caught the keys then rushed to the gate. Wolf moved her hands to her chest then moved her hands down to her stomach. Luis crouched next to Wolf.

"Please show me mercy," she said.

"Why do you deserve mercy," Luis asked her.

"I don't but I feel pain in my stomach," Wolf said.

"Well I did shoot you there," Luis said with a sigh.

"Just show me mercy," she whimpered.

"Answer my questions then I will," he said as he looked back at the gate.

"Okay," she said.

"How many of you are there," Luis asked.

"We have ten men and women," she said as more blood squirted out of her arm.

"What buildings are they in," he asked as he looked at the knife in his hand.

"One is in the auditorium. Another is in the cafeteria. The last five are in the one hundred building." Wolf said as she lifted her head to look at Skeleton.

"Thank you Wolf," Luis said as he moved the knife to her throat.

Luis stabbed Wolf's throat then cleaned the knife's blade on her shirt. Milena threw the keys near him. She waved bye to him before the gate closed. Luis put both bodies in the golf cart. Luis picked up the keys, pistols, and axe. He stopped walking to the auditorium as sirens went off in the parking lot. As Luis walks thunder started to go off in the sky. Small drops of rain started to wash away blood. Inside the auditorium drama students hid. A man with a dragon mask covering his face walked through the audience's seat. He whistled a small spine crawling tune. A small boy rocked himself back and forth crying.

"I don't even go to this school. I'm just a shadow for the day. Why is this even happening?" The boy said to himself.

The boy jumped when the door next to him opened. Luis put the axe in the doorway to keep it open. He looked at the students holding each other. Luis crouched next to them.

"I'm going to get you out of here. You just have to trust me." Luis whispered to them.

Luis stands and walked to the middle of the stage. He watched the man walk around with a blue assault rifle in his hands. The whistle from Luis made the man look at him.

"Are you kid, ready to die," the man asked.

"No, I'm here to join your cause," Luis said with a fake smile.

"Well then welcome aboard kid," the man said.

"Thank you, sir," Luis said with the smile still on his face.

"My name is Dragon and nice jacket. Did you get it from the girl in the gym?" Dragon said as he stopped walking.

"Yes, I did," Luis responded in a growl.

"Did you like how many times I shot her," Dragon asked with a small laugh.

"No because I had to watch her die in my arms," Luis said angrily.

"Oh good," Dragon said.

"Oh, the kids are right here." Luis said while pointing to the right side of the stage.

Dragon ran up to the stage with a smile. Luis stepped to the side allowing him to pass. Dragon aimed at the twenty students.

Luis pulled the pistol out and aimed at the man's knees. He fired two shots then aimed higher. Dragon fell to his knees with a small scream. Luis aimed at his back and emptied the clip in Dragon's back. Dragon started to gasp for air while Luis unsheathed his knife.

"This is for my sister Desiree," Luis screamed.

Luis started to stab Dragon repeatedly in the neck. The students watched Luis almost decapitate Dragon. Luis stopped to clean the blood off his face and glasses. He sheathed the knife then looked at the students.

"Out the door and run to the gate. Don't stop for a single thing. Now move." Luis ordered.

All the students thanked Luis as they ran out the door. Luis dragged Dragon's body to the golf cart. After putting him on the golf cart Luis turned around to see students jumping the fence. He ran to the gate as two helicopters flew overhead. One helicopter circled the auditorium. Luis unlocked the gate and let all the students out. He left the gate open as he ran back to the golf cart. Luis got in the golf cart and started to drive.

"You all have been gathered here for the finale game. This game is called sword fight. One of you will fight one of us with that katana on the floor. If you refuse you'll be shot and killed." A man said with amusement.

Luis pulled up to see four women and a guy standing behind another guy. He quietly knocked all the other dead bodies on the ground. As he put them on the floor he saw other dead bodies. Students lay ripped to pieces by bullets or other weapons. Teachers and security guards lay on the floor in the same state as the students.

"Now who is going to go first? Come on, come fight Swords Master." The man said with his hands extended.

A tall girl with blonde hair and green eyes stepped forward.

Some girl in the crowed of students yelled, "Lily no!"

Lily picked up the katana then looked at Swords Master. Luis crouched down behind the golf cart with the assault rifle aimed at the school shooters. As Swords Master moved forward Luis opened fire. Lily jumped back as two bodies hit the floor. The assault rifle stopped working.

"You idiots come get me," Luis yelled.

Luis stepped out from behind his cover with his other pistol drawn. Rain started to pore down. Lily and Swords Master fight while Luis killed two more people. Lightning struck a tree setting it a flame. Luis tossed the pistol aside then ran at the girl. Her eyes widened behind her owl mask. Luis unsheathed his knife. The girl unsheathed two knives while running at Luis.

"Owl don't kill him. When I kill this girl, I'll end his life." Swords Master yelled.

"Yes, Swords Master," Owl responded.

Owl swung wildly at Luis. Luis dodged then cut her arm. She swung at Luis then got hit in return. Step after step they got closer to the burning tree. Luis kicked Owl into the tree and watched her catch on fire. She screamed in pain as she ran. Luis glanced at the tree. The tree fell on top of her. Luis ran over to stab her in the head. Her screams stopped and another filled the air. Lily lay on the floor holding her side. Swords Master raised his sword over his head. Luis started running at full speed then stopped to throw the knife. Swords Master screamed as the knife entered his back. Luis ran to Lily's side. He kneeled next to her and looked at her wound.

"I'll be fine just finish what you started," Lily said.

"I promise I'll get you out of here," Luis responded.

"Look out," Lily said.

Luis turned in time to put his hand up. The katana cut Luis's hand. Swords Master searched Luis's face for a look of pain or emotion. Luis grabbed the katana from Lily. He rose to his feet making the katana go deeper into his hand. Swords Master's face changed from angry to pure fear. Blood started to run down Luis's wrist. He swung the sword as soon as he lets the other one go. Swords Master's katana went flying to the side. He started to back away.

"Please don't kill me," Swords Master pleaded.

"It's too late," Luis said.

Luis swung the sword at Swords Master's head. He dropped the sword as Swords Master's head rolled on the floor. Police started running into the court yard with their guns raised.

Everyone on the ground now," an officer screamed.

"Officers that girl needs medical attention. She has taken a swing from a katana to her side. I need a bandage for my hand." Luis said as he dropped to his knees.

One of the officer lifted Lily and told the others to follow. Lights from flashing cameras blind Luis. News reporters started to question students about the attack. Each student pointed at Luis. Luis watched Lily get loaded into an ambulance before sitting on one himself. A medic fixed his hand while Milena held his other hand. Luis looked at Milena watching students being looked at.

"You saved so many lives today Luis," Milena said.

"I didn't save her though," Luis responded with a new tear in his eye.

Milena put her head-on Luis's shoulder as an officer walked up to Luis. Luis looked into the officer's brown eyes, the officer smiled at Luis.

"You saved more lives in one day then I have in a week. This act of bravery will be known forever. You are now famous kid. What's your name?" The officer said as he looked at Luis hand.

"Is the school going to close," Luis asked.

"For a week but then it will reopen since there aren't much schools left because of all the gang attacks. What's your name kid?" The officer said with a smile.

"I am Luis Hernandez the broken hero," Luis said with tears streaming down his face.

The end of part 1

Part 2

In a room with white painted walls a teenage boy at the age of sixteen sat in a brown leather chair. Dark clouds peered through the crystal-clear windows. A black leather jacket with bullet holes lays across the boy's lap. He moved his hand to fix the blue tie he has on. Long black hair fell forward covering his face as he bowed his head. Tears started to stream down his face. A tall man with short black hair and green eyes put down his sketch pad. He got up to hug the teen.

"I'm sorry Jesse Williams but I have to go," the boy said as he stood up.

The boy fixed his suit.

"Wait I'll drive you to her funeral. Why are you calling me by my full name?" Jesse said as he stepped back.

"I don't know. I'm sorry Jesse." The boy said sadly.

"Luis, you know I'm here for you," Jesse said.

Luis nodded as he stood by the door. Jesse grabbed something from his desk then walked to the door. Jesse looked at the leather jacket as he opened the door.

"Are you going to fix that leather jacket," Jesse asked.

Luis shook his head no while he put it on. They walk outside to a black car. Jesse unlocked the doors to his car. Luis and Jesse got in the car. As they drive Jesse turned the radio on to avoid the awkward silence. A few hours pass when rows of gravestones came into view. Jesse parked the car for Luis to climb out.

"Thank you for the ride Jesse," Luis said before closing the car door.

As Jesse drove away Luis looked up at the dark cloudy sky. A short girl with blonde hair and green eyes walked up to him.

"Hey, love they are waiting for you to help carry the casket," the girl said as she opened her umbrella.

Lightning flashed in the sky as rain started to poor down. The girl put a hand on his arm. He looked at her and showed a fake smile.

"I know how much this hurts you Luis. Please take my hand." The girl said holding out her hand.

"I know this isn't the right time Milena but just know I do love you," Luis said.

Milena smiled and pulled him into a hug. She whispered into his ear that she loves him too. They stop hugging each other as a short woman with black hair and brown eyes walked up to them.

"Hello Luis and Milena. Luis my husband and some of the others are waiting for you." The women said.

"I'll hurry over to them then," Luis responded.

Luis left Milena and the women to run over to a white funeral car. The group of men started to take a nice smooth black casket out of the car. One of the men counted to three as they lift the casket over their shoulder. The sound of thunder created a beat for them to walk to. After they put the casket in its place Luis went to sit next to Milena and his dead friend's parents. Luis walked up to the grave and dropped a red rose into the grave. Luis watched it hit the casket then turned to everyone else.

"I'd like to stand here before all of you today to speak in Desiree's loving memory. Every day I would walk into Cardinal High to see my sister. She wasn't blood related but she was and still is my sister and best friend. I liked no matter what you did she would look at you with her brown eyes and smile with the purest joy. When she would get nervous she would wrap her black hair around her index finger." Luis said as tears started to fall from his eyes as he took a breath.

He looked at the women who came up to him earlier and the man next to her. Milena got up from her seat to stand next to Luis. "She would still be here today if I would have gotten to her hiding place faster. I made sure that monster died a horrible death for taking Desiree from us two months ago." Luis said with a little anger in his voice.

Desiree's parents wiped tears from their eyes as Luis and Milena sat back down. Everyone left after the funeral ended. Luis sat in front of his friend's unfinished grave with his head bowed. He clenched his fists as he cried more.

"I should have been there. I could have saved you. Why did they have to take you and not me?" Luis said to himself.

Luis felt a small hand on his shoulder. Milena crouched next to him.

"As long as you hold her in your heart she'll still be with you. At least you got to save me and keep another person you love. Come on it's time for us to leave so they can finish burying Desiree." Milena said gently.

Luis got to his feet then helped Milena to hers. They held hands as they walked to her car. The hum of the engine put Luis to sleep as Milena drove.

Gunfire went off in the warm gentle breeze. Luis grabbed Milena's hand as they ran to the nearest building. Screams filled the air as other students scattered in different directions. Luis stopped running and pulled at the locked doors.

"Hurry they're coming," a girl screamed as the gunfire got closer.

Luis picked up a trash can and threw it through the glass door. Milena and Luis ran into the building. The other students helped Luis put tables to cover the glass doors. Milena let out a scream as a man in a black trench coat threw his entire body through a glass door. A girl got knocked to the floor as he swung an axe. Blood splattered across the room. A male student ran past Luis in fear. The man threw the axe. A small scream left the boy's mouth as he fell to the floor. Luis looked at Milena holding her stomach after a bullet grazed past Luis's cheek. He ran to her to catch her from hitting the hard-cold ground. She lands in his arms. Her lips started to turn blue as tears fell from her eyes. Luis brushed her blonde hair out of her face.

"Luis, I feel cold. Can you keep me warm?" Milena said in pain.

"No, you are going to be fine," Luis whimpered.

"Luis know that I love you with all my heart," Milena said.

Luis laid Milena onto the floor. He put his shaking hands on top of hers to put more pressure on her wound.

"You are not going to leave me," he said before he kissed her.

The man pointed a silver revolver at Milena's head and laughs.

"She already has left you kid," the man said.

Tears fell from Luis's eyes as Milena's blood splattered onto his face. Luis looked the man straight in the face.

"Go ahead and fucking get it over with," Luis screamed at the man.

The sound of the revolver made Luis wake up with a scream. Luis looked at Milena. Luis sat in the passenger seat panting from his nightmare. Milena hugged Luis and didn't want to let him go.

"I know this is going to haunt you for a while. I'm right here if you ever need me." Milena said into Luis ear.

"Can you come in and stay with me? I don't want to be alone," Luis said.

"For you of course. Is your mother still in New York," Milena asked?

"Yep, she is still working with the people of Power Tree," Luis said.

Milena turned the car's engine off in the driveway of a two-story house. They got out of the car and stand in the shadow of the brown house. Luis unlocked the door as news trucks pulled up in front of the house. Luis pushed open the door to the house then turned to face the news reporters. All at once they shouted his name. Milena put out her arm to stop him.

"Don't it's not worth talking to them," she said.

He looked at her and smiled. They enter the house ignoring the reporters. Something up the oak stairs crashed and shattered. Luis ran to the broom closet. He opened the black door to see nothing but dark shapes. Buzzing rung in the closet as the light flicked on. Hanging on the wall is a long archery bow. In a quiver underneath the bow are arrows with black and red feathers. Luis took the quiver and strapped it to his back. He grabbed the bow then ran up the stairs two at a time. He heard someone walking around in his room. Luis drew an arrow and nocked it. Luis kicked open the door scaring the intruder. A skeleton mask covered the intruder's face. Luis pointed the bow at the intruder in anger.

"I don't want to do this today. You can come down stairs and help me by answering my questions. The other choice you have is to run and I kill you. Please choose wisely." Luis told the intruder.

The intruder turned and jumped out the window. Wood and shattered glass follow the intruder down to the grass. Luis sighed as he followed at full speed. As Luis is about to touch the ground he rolled onto his back. He jumped to his feet. The news reporters watch the gate get kicked open. Luis ran behind the mystery person dressed in black.

"Stop or I'll shoot you," Luis screamed.

"You can try," the intruder yelled.

Luis nocked an arrow again. He watched as it flew like a crow flies through the sky. The intruder tumbled and fell with the arrow in their knee. Laying on the floor the intruder pulled out a gun. Another arrow hit the intruder. The person screamed as their arm got nailed into the ground by the arrow. Luis started to stand over the intruder as Milena came running out of the house. He bent over and took off the intruder's mask. Light brown hair covered the girl's face. She shook her head in anger. Her brown eyes stared into Luis's brown eyes.

"I see you got contact lenses brother," the girl said.

"I'm not your brother. What is your name?" Luis barked at her.

"My name is Destiny," she said with a smile.

"Who sent you to my house," Luis asked.

"Our father did," she responded.

Anger built inside Luis as he nocked another arrow.

"What you going to kill you sister," she asked.

"Who sent you," Luis asked.

"Our father," Destiny said with a smile.

Luis released the arrow. Destiny screamed in pain as the arrow nailed her other arm into the ground. Luis lifted up Destiny's leg and grabbed hold of the arrow in her knee.

"Who sent you," Luis asked in anger.

"Our father's gang did," Destiny responded.

"What is this gang," Luis asked.

"Our fathers' gang," she said with a small giggle.

Luis ripped the arrow out of her knee. Destiny screamed in pain. The blood splattered all over Luis. The news reporters stared in shock.

"Who is your father," Luis asked as he turned red with anger.

"You killed our cousin brother," Destiny said.

Luis threw her leg down. She let out a small whimper as he stepped on the leg. He nocked an arrow then aimed at her other leg.

"Give me the right answer," Luis said as spit flew out of his mouth.

"How does it feel to torture your family," she asked.

"You broke into my house then pulled a gun on me. I have a right to do this. Now who sent you?" Luis yelled at her.

"Let's see how you feel when our mother gets here," Destiny said.

Luis released the arrow then nocked another arrow. A mail truck pulled up and a guy climbed out. He walked to Milena giving her a paper to sign. She signed the paper then took the box.

"Open it blonde girl," Destiny said with a smile as the man walked away.

Destiny started to laugh as Milena opened the box. Milena dropped the box with a gasp and tears in her eyes. A head with blonde hair rolled out of the box. Tears fell from Luis's eyes as he looked at his mother's head.

"Hello mother you trader," Destiny said with a laugh.

Luis looked back at Destiny with hatred in his eyes.

"Who killed my mother," Luis asked.

"Our father did. You may be called a hero but you are not a strong one. Our family is strong and never will stop hunting you brother." Destiny yelled with a smile still on her face.

Luis released the arrow. Destiny screamed in pain then laughed. He walked up to her head with a tight grip on his bow.

"Before you kill me I got one last request," she said.

"Speak," Luis barked.

"Can I watch the pretty fireworks," she asked.

"What are you talking about," Luis asked.

"It's good to see you one last time brother," Destiny said.

Luis swung the bow hitting her. He stopped as she turned her bloody face to look at the house.

"Answer me," Luis said.

"You shall see now," Destiny said as she spit out blood.

Luis nocked an arrow. The side of house explodes sending him to the ground. Fire spread across the grass dashing to Destiny. Luis got to his feet feeling heat on his back. He quickly took off his quiver and leather jacket. Luis threw them as they burned to ash. Destiny started to scream as half of her body started to burn. Sirens went off in the distance. Smoke filled the area from the burning grass and house. Luis started to search for Milena as sadness took over his mind.

"Luis where are you," Milena asked.

"I'm over here," Luis yelled back.

"Follow my voice," Milena said.

Luis followed the voice to the street. Milena stood there with blood slowly running down the side of her head. She started to run toward him. Police, paramedics, and firefighters pulled up. They rush out of their vehicles like soldiers running into the face of battle.

Luis and Milena stand in the middle of the commotion hugging each other. Jesse's black car pulled up. He tried to get to Luis but an officer stopped him.

"Ma'am I need you to come with me so I can take care of your head," the paramedic said.

"Sir that officer wants to speak with you," an officer said.

"I'm not leaving her side," Luis responded.

The officer and the paramedic nod then walked in different direction. Milena and Luis followed the paramedic to his ambulance. After ten minutes the firefighters packed up their trucks and start to leave. An officer with short brown hair walked up to Luis and Milena. He pushed up his glasses then smiled.

"I'm sorry for your loss sir. My name is Sargent Evans. For right now I only got one question for you. Do you have a place to stay?" The officer said looking at Milena with a smile.

"He is going to stay with me," Milena said.

"How old are you ma'am," the officer asked.

"I'm sixteen and I live with my mother," Milena said.

"Tomorrow if you are able please come to the station for further questions," the officer said.

Sargent Evans pulled out a card. He looked down at it before handing it to Luis. Luis accepted the card with a fake smile. Sargent Evans walked to his car and drove away.

"So how are we getting to your house," Luis asked.

"I can call my mom," Milena said.

"I'm sorry about your car," Luis said.

"Luis it's not your fault the house exploded. Well only part of your room did." Milena said looking at the house.

Milena put her head on his shoulder. He turned and kissed her head. Jesse walked up to them. Luis and Milena stood up from sitting on sidewalk.

"Jesse I'm sorry but my mom is dead," Luis said.

"Luis I'm sorry this happened to you. You can come stay with me if you want," Jesse said.

"Thank you for the offer but I'm going to stay with my girlfriend. What were you coming to my house for," Luis asked.

"I'm still going to be around for you and to drop these, off." Jesse said as he handed Luis a pair of car keys.

Luis looked at the car keys he took from Jesse.

"It's in the garage," Jesse said as he walked to his car.

Milena took the keys from Luis then ran to the garage. He shook his head then chased after her. She stood in front of the open garage door with her hand over her mouth. Luis walked past Milena in shock. His hand started to shake as he put his hand on the hood of the car. It's shiny red paint reflected the light around the garage.

"This is the car I wanted," Luis said.

"Isn't this the car that came out this year," Milena said.

Luis nodded yes as he looked at her. She walked over to him and grabbed his hand. Milena looked down at the dirt and ash circling a long scar on his palm. She gently placed the car keys in his hand then looked into his eyes.

"Are we going to talk about that day two months ago," Milena asked.

"I will," Luis said.

"When? As of right now your friend Lily is the only one who understands what you did. She is also the only one besides you who knows the entire story." Milena said with a little anger in her voice.

"I don't know when I'll talk about it," Luis said.

"Well these reporters won't stop asking you questions until you agree to talk," Milena said.

"Let them keep coming because the world will know when I'm ready to talk," Luis said.

Milena let out a sigh then looked out the garage. Luis put a hand on her shoulder. She looked back into his eyes.

"Hey, I know you don't like them coming after us every few days. When I'm ready that is when they will get the full story and I'm with you so don't worry about me cheating on you. I'm loyal to you because you are my girlfriend. Before we leave to your house I'm going to scavenge through the house for things I need." Luis said before kissing her forehead gently.

"Then I'll help you. Where do I start?" Milena asked with a fake smile.

"You can start upstairs in my bathroom, my room and the home office. Bring whatever you can down here in this box." Luis said staring into her eyes.

Before Luis moved to grab an empty box and a flashlight Milena kissed him. She smiled then grabbed a box then the flashlight. Luis watched her leave the garage and entered the house. He then unlocked the car's trunk.

"Okay time to clean the garage," he said to himself.

Outside two tall teenage boys in blood stained leather jackets sat on their motorcycles across the street. One moves forward. The other one put an arm out to stop him. They look at each other then back away from the sidewalk.

"We will go meet them tomorrow," one of them said.

"This will be really boring," said the other.

"We have orders to follow them until we get a call for further orders," the other on responded.

"Let's hope it doesn't take long then," the other one said.

Back in the garage Luis opened a large silver brief case with packaging foam. In between the packaging foam are silver knives. Underneath the knives is a belt with knife scabbards attached to it. He closed the brief case then put it in the trunk. Luis went to a big cabinet and sighed. It creaked as the old doors open. Luis smiled as he pulled out four duffel bags.

"It's a good thing none of these bags are empty," he said while placing them in the trunk.

He unzipped the bags to see two bags full of revolver rounds and the other two full of money. He zipped the bags closed then went back to the cabinet. A small chirping went off as his pocket vibrated. Luis pulled out his smartphone to see the name mom on the phone's contact id. He ran out of the garage to the living room.

Luis pulled a phone charger out of its plug and turned on an open laptop on a small wooden coffee table. The phone continued to ring as Luis opened up a file on the desktop.

"Come on you god damn file open," Luis said to the computer.

A small box popped up on the screen. Luis plugged the phone into the cord connected to the laptop. He answered the phone as a map popped up on the screen tracing the call.

"Hello," Luis said.

"Hello Luis Hernandez. I know you think your mother is working but it's now a lie," a man said.

"Who are you," Luis asked.

"Your mother and uncle haven't told you," the man said.

The computer said fifty percent complete as the voice let out a sigh.

"That doesn't surprise me. I am your father and I want you to come home. Come home to me my dragon child." The man said happily.

"You listen to me. I'm not your son and you are not my father. All my family is dead and you killed them. So, you know Destiny is going back to you in a body bag." Luis said angrily.

"You killed my daughter and your sister," the man said.

"Stop telling me lies. I'll find you and I'll kill you and who ever stands in my way. Everyone who works for you will die. I won't stop till my mother's killers meet their death. I hope you say good bye to everyone you love because you are going to be the last person to die." Luis said with anger in his voice.

"We'll be together soon then," the man said.

The man hung up the phone. Luis yelled out in frustration as the computer lost the trace. Luis took the phone off the cord and called Jesse.

"Hello Luis," Jesse said.

"Can you do me a favor," Luis asked.

"Yes, I can. What is it?" Jesse asked with concern in his voice.

"All the televisions, the washer and drier is what I need removed and kept safe. Can you come get them and keep them at your house?" Luis asked Jesse.

"Yes," Jesse said.

"Thank you, Jesse. This helps a lot." Luis said before hanging up the phone.

Luis texted someone named Lily, then closed the laptop and put it in the back seat of the car with its charger. The phone rang again in his pocket. A picture of a girl with blonde hair and green eyes smiling next to Luis popped up on his phone. In white letters the name Lily appeared above her head.

"What do you need," Lily asked.

"I'm going to need your help with something. Can you meet me at Quinn's café in two hours?" Luis asked her.

"Yes, I might be late though," Lily said.

"That is fine. I just need you to be there," Luis said.

"Okay, see you then," Lily said.

He hung up the phone and put it in his pocket. Luis pulled a small brief case with packaging foam in it and put it in the trunk open. As he grabbed two revolvers from the cabinet the stairs started to creek. He dashed to the trunk and put them in the case.

"I found a lot of things intact. I couldn't open the safe so I brought it down here. All of your other things are by the stairs." Milena said with a smile.

"You are joking about the safe," Luis asked.

"Yes, I'm joking. I'm strong but not that strong." Milena said playfully.

She stood in the door way smiling. They started to put three boxes full of books in the trunk. Milena put the three laptops she found on top of the other one.

"Did you get the suitcase next to the desk with all the laptop stuff in it," Luis asked.

"No," Milena responded.

"Can you get it and the money from inside the wall safe? The code is 2416." Luis asked Milena.

Luis handed her six empty duffel bags. Milena took them then went up the stairs. Luis opened a cabinet. He looked at the twenty quivers full off arrows hanging on hooks. One by one he placed them in the trunk. After putting his red bow in the trunk he looked at a sword with a dragon on the hilt. Luis picked it up and put it in the trunk. He closed the trunk before entering the house. Something in the kitchen beeped. Luis ran to the kitchen to see the drier's green light flashing. He turned to the kitchen sink to wash off his hands and face. A dog barked outside at the dark sky. Luis opened the drier to see clean clothes in it. He smiled then took them out. Luis walked to the bathroom to change. Milena walked down the stairs with her hands full. Luis walked out of the bathroom dressed in a black shirt and navy blue jeans. He looked at Milena and smiled.

"I almost forgot to check your bathroom. All of your stuff is in this duffel bag. You have a lot of money in that safe." Milena said.

"I know. All that money was saved over the years by my mom." Luis said with a smile.

Milena walked to the car to load what she brought down into the back seat of the car. Luis walked over to the broom closet. The buzzing from the light continued as Luis grabbed a pair of black sneakers. He put on his socks and shoes. Before leaving he grabbed a black baseball hat and a black trench coat. After putting them on he noticed a holstered pistol on a shelf. Luis grabbed it and strapped it to his belt. He got in the car and started it.

"What are you going to do for clothes," Milena asked.

"After I drop you off at your house I'm going to go shopping. I'll only be an hour or two." Luis said with Lily on his mind.

"Okay," Milena said.

In a small coffee shop sitting in a corner with four laptops in front of him is Luis. He looked up at the brown goldish walls. People passed by ordering coffee or their comic book themed donuts. The bell on the door rang as a girl with blonde hair walked in. Luis watched her as he drank some of his hot tea. Her green eyes locked onto his brown eyes as she walked over to him.

"You look like one of those beautiful elves from the movies," Luis said.

"You keep talking like that and I'll have to steal you from Milena," Lily said.

"Funny, I would like to see that happen. So, you ready to work," Luis asked.

"What are we working on," Lily asked.

"We are going to hack into every single camera in New York City to see who fought and killed my mother," Luis said.

"Luis, we don't need to do that," Lily said.

"What are you talking about," Luis asked.

Lily sat in front of a laptop and pulled up a website. She faced the screen toward Luis.

"This building is the headquarters of every single camera on the streets of New York. All I need to do is get into their network and look at the recorded files around the hotel," Lily said.

"So that means all I need to do is get into the hotel's security cameras," Luis said.

"What is the name of the hotel," Lily asked.

"It's the Warm Harley Palace. You take those two laptops and I'll take these two." Luis said with a smile.

"That's one fancy hotel," Lily said with a smile.

Lily and Luis set to work for an hour. Luis looked over at Lily as she was going through footage of tapes. He thought of kissing her lips and holding her in his arms. Luis stopped looking at her then pulled up two screens. One dealt with the lobby of the hotel and the other is pointed down a hallway.

"I've got what I need," Luis said.

"I think I found the footage outside," Lily said.

"I'll play mine then play yours," Luis responded.

Lily and Luis watched the soundless footage in the lobby. A group of twenty men walked in through the doors. People started to jump over chairs and tables. They all hid in terror as the men pulled out guns. Luis watched as they made their way to the elevator. Luis switched laptops then hit play.

"That is so weird," Luis said.

"What is," Lily asked.

"That man is a police officer," Luis said as he zoomed in on a man with glasses and short brown hair.

As the camera zoomed out to show the entire hallway Luis was on the other laptop. The man's face popped up on the screen. The name Brian Evans popped up next to his face.

"This officer was at my house today and at our school the day I killed all of the school shooters. I'm going to see him at the police station tomorrow." Luis said to Lily.

"That scumbag. Luis look," Lily said.

Luis looked back at the camera footage to see the door get blown open. Six men and women jumped out of the door with fire and ice shooting out of their hands. Sargent Evans got kicked to the floor as Luis's mom ran out of the room. She fired a couple of shots at the men then ran to the elevator. Three of those men and women jumped into the elevator with his mom. Lily covered her mouth as the three that stayed got killed. Sargent Evans and his living ten men ran to the stairs. Lily switched cameras back to the lobby while Luis shut down the other one.

"Who are those people she is with," Lily asked.

"I don't know for sure. I think they work with her." Luis said.

Luis's mother and her companions burst out of the elevator. Two of her companions took bullets to the head. Luis's mother and her friend ran outside. Lily played her camera footage. Luis's mother stopped running as more men stand outside waiting. Luis's mother's friend got shot as Sargent Evans walked outside. Evans looked into the camera and shot it.

"That fucking bastard is going to die. I'm going to kill him," Luis said angrily.

"You can't just walk into a police station and shoot him," Lily said.

"There are other ways Lily," Luis said.

"If you are going to hunt these killers down then I'm going to help you. Don't say no. You know I can help because I'm more qualified than anyone else." Lily said.

"Why do you want to help," Luis asked.

"You are my friend and I want to help you because you would do the same if it were me," Lily said.

"Good to know you are up for getting your hands dirty," Luis said.

"To help end those horrible people, of course," Lily responded.

"I'll see you at school tomorrow," Luis said.

After logging out of the computers and shutting them down Luis hugged Lily. Before Lily let go of Luis she gave him a kiss on the cheek.

"I love you Luis," Lily said.

Luis hesitated to say something.

"Be safe out there," Lily said with a smile.

"You to kid," Luis said.

Lily smiled as Luis started to pack up to leave the café. Luis looked to see her by the café door. She blew him a kiss before leaving. Luis smiled as he collects his things. Luis walked to his car to drive to Milena's house.

"I need to talk to Jesse after the police station tomorrow," Luis thought.

Luis awakened to the smell of scrambled eggs, bacon and cinnamon toast. He rubbed his eyes as he walked to the stairs. Each step creaked as he walked up them. The door opened to show Milena in the door way.

"Morning," Luis said.

"Good morning to you love," Milena said.

"Come on you two," a woman yelled.

"Coming mother," Milena said.

They walked into the blue and white dining room. Milena sat on a brown Mexican wooden chair. A tall woman with green eyes and blonde hair put plates of food on the table. She looked at Luis and gave him a smile.

"Sit down you need to eat. So how did you sleep?" the women said.

"I didn't sleep well last night," Luis responded.

"Are you still having those nightmares," Milena asked.

"Only when I think of that day. Thank you for letting me stay here Mrs. Pool." Luis said with a smile.

"You are welcome. If you need anything else let me know. No one should be going through what you are," Mrs. Pool said.

Luis came down the stairs from a nice shower. He went down to the basement to get his things then walked up stairs. He kissed Milena before she walked out the door. Luis walked outside after Milena. After Mrs. Pool locked the door, the phone rang and she dashed off to answer it.

"Hello," Mrs. Pool said.

"Did they leave yet," a man asked.

"Yes, they did. The mission is a go then," She asked.

"It's always been a green light," the man said.

Mrs. Pool hang up the phone then walked to the kitchen.

"Let the fun begin," Mrs. Pool said with a smile.

Luis pulled up in front of a large square shaped building. A silver sign sat on top of three rocks. In green letters on the sign read Echo Police department. He entered through the double glass doors with a smile. A voice echoed around the orange room. Luis turned to his left to see an old woman. She pushed her glasses up then smiled as she looked at Luis. Luis pulled out Sargent Evans card then slid it under the bullet proof glass.

"What do you need from Sargent Evans sir," the women asked.

"He told me to stop by to answer some questions," Luis said.

"Okay, I'll need your name sir," she asked.

"Luis Hernandez," Luis said with a smile.

"Are you the Luis that saved your school," the women asked.

"Yes I am." Luis said with a frown.

"You have inspired my grandson to join the army. I wanted to thank you for that." She said with a smile.

"You are welcome," Luis said a little bit confused.

"Please wait here and I'll go get him," she said.

The old women got up then walked away from the window. Luis sat down on the bench in front of the window. The women came back to the window and smiled.

"He'll be with you in two seconds," she said with a smile.

Luis got to his feet as Sargent Evans stepped into the waiting room. A large pile of files was under one of his arms. Evans smiled as he gestured for Luis to follow him.

"I didn't expect you until this afternoon," Evans said.

"I don't have classes until twelve," Luis said.

"That girl you were next to yesterday is very pleasing to the eye," Evans said.

"That is my girlfriend," Luis said.

They stopped in front of a glass room. Evans opened the door to the room. Luis sat in a plastic chair with a metal table in front of him. Evans sat down then slid the files to Luis. Luis read the title of the file then looked at Evans. He pointed at the file for Luis to read. Luis picked up the pictures under the file. The memory of pinning Destiny with arrows entered his mind. In the photo, it showed half of her body burnt. The other half of her body was undamaged by the flames. Luis put the photo down then looked at the other photo. Destiny's arm lay on a metal table. A tattoo of a dragon flying toward the name Luis showed on her wrist. Luis looked at another photo of a wolf on fire tattooed to her back. Luis put the photo of Destiny's cleaned dead body aside. He picked up the photos of his mother's head. Tears fill his eyes as he put the photos down.

"Did you find her body," Luis asked.

"No. We have officers looking for a body without a head in New York," Evans said.

"I never said where she was," Luis said.

Luis made a face at Evans. He nodded then looked at the file.

Luis put Destiny's autopsy report aside then looked at the file that said Fire Wolves in black shiny letters. Luis closed the file and slid it to Evans. Evans picked up the file and read it aloud.

"The head of this gang is Luke Hernandez. He is married to Zamora Hernandez. He has a scar on his left eye and is five foot six. Has brown hair and green eyes. Luke is Hispanic. Luke claims he and his Fire Wolves are the kings of crime. His three kids are Luis Hernandez, Destiny Hernandez, and Eric Hernandez."

"I don't have any siblings or a father. I'm a bastard," Luis said.

Sargent Evan sighed then started to read again.

"Luke Hernandez has a brother named Jesse Williams. I know this is a shock to you but it's true. This file was my father's till he passed it to me nine years ago. Are you still in contact with them," Evans asked with some anger in his voice.

"No," Luis said.

"Why are they attacking you," Evans asked.

"I don't know," Luis said.

"You do know. You interrogated your sister," Evans said with anger in his voice.

"Now that I think of it I do know," Luis said.

"Please share," Evans said as he crossed his arms.

"They are after me because of what I did at the school. Then you went after my mother and killed her," Luis said.

"We can protect you," Evans said with a smile.

"No, you won't. I know you won't because your one of them," Luis said as he got up.

Luis walked out of the room. He walked to his car and saw someone on a motorcycle. Sargent Evans came running out of the building. Luis opened his car door. Evans stepped in front of Luis's car as he started the engine.

"Get out of the way," Luis ordered.

"No, we'll get you sooner or later. If you want it to be difficult then your life will be a living hell." Evans said with a smile.

"The day I get taken is the time I'm the last thing you see again," Luis said with a smile.

Luis started to drive away making Evans jump out of the way. Evans looked at the person on the motorcycle and nodded his head yes. He watched as the motorcycle started to follow Luis. Evans ran back in the building.

"This kid has no idea what he is fighting against," Evans said to himself.

Luis parked in the stone drive way. He grabbed a notepad from the back seat. Luis got out of the car. A light brown house sat in place blocking out the sun. The front door opened and Jesse walked out of the house.

"Luis what is going on," Jesse asked.

"I need to talk to you," Luis said.

"Well let's go inside then," Jesse said.

Luis followed Jesse into the house. The door closed as a person on a motorcycle pulled up. They took off their helmet. Black and green hair fell onto their shoulders. They pulled out a phone.

"I got a green light from Evans," they said.

"What do you need," a man asked.

"Get twenty men to the school to look for Milena," they said.

"It will be done," the man said.

In the house, Luis sat at a nice wooden table writing two letter addressed to Milena and Lily. As he finished Jesse came to the table with two cups of tea in his hands. Luis took a cup then waited for Jesse to sit down.

"What is it you need child," Jesse asked.

"I know I've asked you so much already but I got two more things for you to do." Luis said as he looked at the letters.

"It's fine. Whatever you need I'm happy to help," Jesse said with a smile.

"Well I need you to be a messenger for me. I need you to give Milena this letter if anything ever happens to me and this one to my friend Lily." Luis said sliding the letters over to Jesse.

"I can do that, is there something else," Jesse asked.

Luis drank some of his tea before looking at Jesse.

"Why are you helping me so much," Luis asked.

"I made a promise to your mom that I would always be here whenever you need something if something ever happened to her," Jesse said with tears in his eyes.

"How did you know you loved my mother," Luis asked.

"I just saw her and knew I loved her. Why are you asking?" Jesse said as he wiped his eyes.

"I just want to know why you were helping me and I needed some advice on love," Luis said.

"Do you love Milena or someone else," Jesse asked.

"I lied to Milena saying I love her because I'm not sure how to end our relationship," Luis said.

"Is there someone else you have feelings for," Jesse asked.

Luis nodded his head yes.

"What kind of feelings do you have for her," Jesse asked.

"I can't get her out of my mind. I can't stop wanting to be with her every single minute of the day. Everything I do now is for Lily and everything I do it's like I can feel her presence next to me." Luis said with a small smile.

"Then you love her," Jesse said.

"How do you know," Luis asked.

"That's how I feel with your mother. Just know you must follow your heart and do what is right for Lily and you. Following your heart is the only way you can have a future with her if that is what you want. Following your heart isn't only just for love it's also for things you believe in." Jesse said as he picked up his tea cup.

Jesse finished drinking his tea as someone started shooting at his front door. Luis and Jesse jumped to their feet.

"Do you have a gun," Luis asked.

"Not in this house, do you have one," Jesse asked.

"In my car," Luis said.

"I may have something for you to use," Jesse said.

Jesse grabbed what Luis gave him and put it in his pocket. Two silver objects sat on a shelf in the hallway. Jesse grabbed them down then grabbed a trench coat. Luis watched as Jesse came back to him. Jesse grabbed his wrists and put the silver objects on him. Luis looked at both of his wrists.

"What are these," Luis asked.

"They are hidden blades," Jesse responded.

Jesse handed Luis the trench coat then showed him how to release the blades and retract them. Luis put the trench coat on as Jesse looked at the door.

"Do you remember what I taught you," Jesse asked.

"Yes," Luis responded.

"Good now you are going to fight in the dark with very little light," Jesse said.

Luis nodded as Jesses ran down a hallway. Within five seconds the house got completely dark, Luis ran to the front living room, he jumped over the couch and laid flat against the carpet. Finally, the intruder stuck their hand through the freshly made hole in the door. The sound of the door slamming against the wall echoed through the house. The intruder walked into the house reloading their shotgun. Luis started to remember how the day started at Cardinal High.

Luis watched as students ran for their lives. Blood splattered across the floor. Limbs flew as an axe chopped them off. Luis jumped over a table to take cover from the bullets. He looked over to see a three-year-old girl crying with her mother's blood splattered on her. Before Luis could move to grab the girl, she hit the floor as her brain matter spread across the grass, other students covered their mouths with tears in their eyes. Luis could see the fear taking over their minds as bodies landed around them. When the gunfire stopped, Luis got up and ran. He jumped through an open-door way. He looked to see Milena and Desiree hiding behind a trophy case. They got up and ran with Luis to the band room. Gunfire went off again after they entered the band room. Before the memory faded Luis looked around for Desiree and didn't see her. Luis came back to the present as the intruder started to talk.

"Come on Luis I know you are here. Don't be a coward. Come and fight me. You weren't afraid to kill your sister so why be afraid now?" The intruder said with a laugh.

The attacker walked past the couch. Luis got up and jumped at the attacker. The click of the hidden blade being released made the attacker smile. Luis stabbed the attackers back then grabbed hold of the helmet. Luis retracted a blade as he took the helmet off then used the helmet to hit them in the head. Luis let the intruder go then threw the helmet outside.

"You're a girl," Luis said.

"Is that a problem," the girl asked.

"No, was hoping you were Brian Evans," Luis said.

"Sorry to disappoint. The name is Starlight," she said.

"Nice to know," Luis said.

"You better hope you survive this. It would be a shame if you died and she died," Starlight said with a smile.

"You talk too much and give away too much information," Luis said while hiding in the shadows.

"What are you talking about," Starlight said.

"You are talking about my girlfriend," Luis said."

"So, you are smart as Evans said," Starlight said.

Luis came out of the shadows and sliced her face then kicked her to the floor. Starlight slowly got to her knees then got knocked to the floor again.

"Why don't you turn the lights on and we'll talk," Starlight asked.

"Not falling for that trick," Luis said.

Luis let her get to her feet then stood behind her. Starlight shot in front of her. Luis made a ticking sound then stabbed her leg.

"If you were a great hit girl you'd be able to listen for me in the dark. If all your good at is shooting a gun then you are nothing." Luis said with a smile.

Xavier L Hernandez

Starlight yelled in frustration as she spun in a circle firing the shotgun. Luis laid flat against the floor.

"My men will kill that girl today at your school," she said while reloading the shotgun again.

Luis got onto his feet then smiled.

"Jesse hit the lights," Luis called.

The lights turned on one by one as Luis knocked her feet from under her. She fell forward. Luis put a hand around her throat. Starlight opened her mouth to speak. She widened her eyes as Luis's blade went through her throat. Blood poured out of her mouth as her eyes rolled to the back of her head. Luis retracted the hidden blade as Jesse came out of the hallway. Luis faced Jesse with a rising fire in his eyes.

"I need to leave now," Luis told him.

"There are things I have to tell you first," Jesse said.

"Tell me in the car. I have to save her from them," Luis said to him.

Luis picked up the shotgun and handed it to Jesse. Luis looked at Jesse with a cold hard stare. He took the gun then followed Luis to the car. They entered the car and Luis pulled out of the drive way.

"Luis, you must know who your blood belongs to. You need to know who me and your mother are," Jesse said.

"I'm listening but speak fast," Luis said.

"It started with two brothers. Those brothers are me and your father. Your father is Luke Hernandez. He is the leader of the Fire Wolves. The gang was called Wolves when my father was in charge. The name changed because we united with another gang. Your mother came from that gang. The gang was called Fire Strike. To seal that boned together was a marriage between your father and mother. That's why it's called Fire Wolves now." Jesse said as he looked out the window.

"That's stupid," Luis said.

"Years later your father became leader, and your mother had

you and Destiny then was pregnant with Eric nine months later," Jesse said.

"So, Destiny was my twin sister," Luis asked.

"Yes. I then became the hitmen of the gang so I was hardly around. After two months, I finally met your mother. We fell in love instantly. We made a plan to steal money and you away from this gang." Jesse said with a small smile.

"Why did you train me to fight and hack into things," Luis asked.

Jesse let out a sigh.

"Your father didn't care that you left. He started to care when an oracle told him his future. He loved Greek culture so much he made sure an oracle was put in the gang." Jesse said after another sigh.

"What did the oracle say and how do you know how to fight more than these other hitmen or hit girls," Luis asked.

"The gang will fall at the hands of a dragon. There would be a time that a male dragon will either join and destroy the Fire Wolves enemies or he destroys the Fire Wolves. He sent people after you to find and bring you back to him. I killed them after interrogating them. Me and your mother made the choice to have you learn what I knew because of your superhuman ability. I am highly trained because I took lesson in every martial arts before I became the hitman. My father wanted the most powerful hitman so he put me in all of those classes. I learned how to hack and do all kinds of other things that you know how to do from my friend that was in the special forces." Jesse said with seriousness in his voice.

Luis turned a corner then looked at Jesse.

"What are you talking about," Luis asked.

"Power Tree is an army of superhumans. After your mother found out that you were part of the superhumans she tracked them down. Since then she has been working with them. Your ability allows you to do great things with your mind." Jesse said as Luis looked back at the road.

"Kind of makes sense." Luis said while thinking of the lights flickering when he screamed after Desiree's death and the tree falling on that school shooter when he looked at it.

Luis pulled into the school parking lot and parked the car. Jesse left the shotgun in the car and got out with Luis. Luis popped open the trunk while he took off the trench coat. He threw it in the trunk. Jesse looked down at the sword Luis reached for. Luis put the sword on his back. Luis closed the trunk then went to the passenger's side of the car. He unlocked the door and grabbed a holstered pistol out of the glove compartment. Jesse watched Luis attach it to his belt.

"You don't have to do this alone," Jesse said.

"I'm not alone. I have you to help protect Lily and Milena. Hide the car and keep it safe for me. Might need it in case of an emergency.

Luis handed him the keys then ran off to the school's building. He walked through the brightly lit building. Students looked at him and smile. Some clap, whistle and shout. Luis stopped walking as Lily ran to him. Her eyes looked at the sword then the gun. She finally gazed into his eyes.

"What's wrong," Luis asked.

"There are people calling your name. Ten of them went to look for Milena." Lily said with a look of concern.

"Are they armed," Luis asked.

"All twenty of them are," Lily responded.

"Show me to the first ten then go find Milena," Luis said.

Lily nodded then started walking to the exit. They walked out to the courtyard with tables full of scared and quiet students. Luis saw the men armed with baseball bats, knives, and guns. Lily ran off as Luis walked up to the officer pointing a gun at the armed men. Luis put a hand on her arm and shook his head no.

"We don't need to lose another one of you good officers today. I got this one. You need to get everyone else to safety." Luis said while looking at the students.

The officer nodded and holstered her pistol.

"All of you students need to go in the one hundred building," the officer said.

One of the men moved his gun to point at the officer. She fell to the floor with blood splattering all over the floor. Luis looked to see blood leaking from the officer's head. One of the men with a bloodstained leather jacket laughed as he licked his pistol.

"Any of you students move you die and become mine and my brother's dinner. Now where is Luis Hernandez and Milena Pool?" One of the men yelled.

None of the students said a single word. The man let out a happy chuckle as he pointed the gun at a student.

"You have till the count of three to tell me where they are or one of you dies," the man said.

Luis un-holsters his pistol and points it at the man.

"One, two, three. Now you die little boy," the man said.

The sound of a gunshot filled the once quiet air. All the men turned around to face Luis. Another man with a bloodstained leather jacket stared Luis down.

"You killed my brother," a man yelled as he ran at Luis.

Luis opened fire on the man. Small amounts of blood sprinkled from his body. Luis used his last bullet to kill the man. He tossed the gun to the side then threw the holster.

"Who are you boy," a woman asked.

"I'm the one and only Luis Hernandez. Now come get me." Luis yelled.

Luis unsheathed his sword as they all charge Luis. He dodged a swing then swung back. A man screamed as Luis chopped off his four fingers. The students started to chant Luis's name. A man aimed a gun at Luis. Luis kicked the other man to the floor then threw his sword. The others backed away in fear as the man aiming at Luis fell to the floor with the sword in his throat.

"You can all leave with your lives still intact," Luis said.

The men ran forward letting yells leave their mouths. Luis released the hidden blades as he charged at them. Each blow thrown at Luis got blocked. Luis stabbed a guy in the eye while he stabbed another in the throat. Luis ducked as someone swung his sword at his head. He retracted the blades to punch a man then disarmed the one with his sword. The students backed away as a head landed next to them.

"Enough of the bloodshed. Luis come with us or she dies." Someone said.

Luis looked up to see ten men standing with Lily and Milena at gun point. Evans stood in his police uniform smiling. Luis moved to walk toward Evans. The two men left from Luis's fight moved to grab him. Luis swung his sword. They hit the floor headless. Evans slapped Milena with the pistol making her fall to the floor. Lily tried to move but stopped as another gun got pointed at her.

"Don't touch Lily," Luis screamed.

"Oh, how sweet of you to care about her," Evans said.

"I swear I'll kill you," Luis said.

"They'll live if you do as I say," Evans said.

"What do you want," Luis asked.

"First throw your sword to the side. Then get on your knees." Evans ordered.

Luis threw his sword to the side then got to his knees. Milena lifted her head while putting a hand to her face. Evans walked up to Luis. He put the gun against Luis's head.

"Oh I'm really going to ignore your father's orders," Evans said.

Luis looked at Lily. Her eyes filled with tears. Luis gave her a smile. Evans put his finger on the trigger. Luis moved his head. His ears started to ring as he got to his feet. Luis and Evans started fighting for the gun. Evans started winning the fight. One of the men standing next to Lily ran toward Luis. The ringing in Luis's ears stopped. Evans stopped laughing as Luis bites his throat. Luis turned to spit out blood and parts of Evans throat. Blood shot out of Evans throat as he fell to the floor. Luis wiped blood from his mouth.

"Like I said to you earlier, I was going to kill you. Say hello to my sister for me." Luis said in a growl.

The life left Evans's eyes as the blood stopped squirting out of his throat. Luis got hit by the butt of a rifle knocking him out. The last thing Luis saw and heard was Lily trying to run to his side and Milena smiling as she punched Lily.

"Take her with you guys," Milena said.

Luis awakened in a metal chair with his hands chained behind his back. A lamp swung back and forth from the ceiling. Luis looked around in the darkness surrounding him. He heard metal clicks and an old door open. Footsteps echoed in the room. A large warm hand touched Luis's hair.

"So, strong and brave," a man said.

"If you want to see how strong I am take off these chains and let's go a few rounds," Luis said.

The hand slapped Luis. He licked his lips as blood dripped down from his lip. Screeches of old rusted wheels came into the room. Luis looked up to see a flat screen television in front of him. The television turned on and showed Milena's face. No tears left her eyes as she looked at the camera. A smile showed on her face. Luis saw a strange face of a liar that has been waiting to reach the surface.

"This attack was to come get my boyfriend Luis Hernandez. He let them take him to save our fellow students. You who call him a coward are cowards. He is a hero that you don't see in people anymore. I'll never stop looking for him." Milena said.

"She is such a great actress. While you have been at your high school brother she has been working for us. So, tell me how does she taste?" The boy said in Luis's ear.

Luis bowed his head and waits for the person who brought the television in to pass. He tipped the chair over and the person jumped back.

"Pick him back up Lily." The man ordered.

Lily picked up Luis and put a couple of paper clips in his hand.

"Come here Lily. I want you to be my second wife even though my first one isn't dead yet." The man said with a smile.

"Whatever you say Eric," Lily said.

Lily kissed Eric while Luis quickly unlocked the chains then dropped them on the floor. Eric slapped Lily's ass as Luis stood up then grabbed the chains. Luis whistled as they stopped kissing. Luis smiled as Lily kneed Eric in the stomach. A small sound of pain left Eric's mouth.

"You bitch that hurt," Eric screamed.

"Next time don't slap my ass," Lily said.

"There won't be a next," Luis said.

Eric looked to see Luis swing the chain at him. Eric spit out blood after Luis hit him. Eric grabbed hold of the chain and tried to pull Luis. Luis let go of the chain then grabbed the chair. Lily punched Eric's nose. Eric ignores Luis and jumped at Lily. Punches flew at Lily while she smiled. She blocked every punch then returned five punches. Eric put a hand to his bloody nose. He then pulled out a pistol. Luis threw the chair at Eric making him lose the gun.

"Dad come meet the lost son. Come meet our dragon." Eric yelled.

Footsteps echoed down the hallway after his call. Luis and Lily teamed up kicking and punching Eric. Luis grabbed his arm and broke it. Eric screamed out in pain as Lily broke the other arm. Eric dropped to his knees with cuts and bruises on his face. He spit out blood as Luis picked up the gun. A short man with silver hair and a scar on his left eye stood in the door way. His green eyes stared at Luis and Lily. Luis put the gun against Eric's head.

"You move and I kill him," Luis said.

"He is weak and useless," the man said.

"Father you can't do this to me. I'm your son. Cassie will help kill you." Eric screamed.

"No, you are not. My son is the one pointing a gun at your head. You are just a replacement. Cassie is someone that I don't fear." The man said with a smile.

The man took a step forward. Eric's dead body hit the floor scaring the man. Luis pointed the gun at the man. He put his hands up.

"I like how you feed the hunger to kill. The year of the dragon suits you. It's good to see you my son. I told you we would be together soon." The man said with a smile.

Luis moved his aim to his father's head. Lily watched Luis as he pulled the trigger. The man laughed as Luis pulled out the pistol's clip.

"Good just good. You really are my son. You have lost so much but gained much more. You don't hesitate to kill and you protect your own. As for the girl, next to you she is going to die." The man said with a smile.

Luis stepped in front of Lily as he put the empty clip back into the gun.

"You have to go through me to kill her," Luis said.

"Then she lives because you say so. Now let's go talk to my oracle." The man said.

"Where is my mother's body and how did you know, my mother was in New York," Luis asked.

"With the fishes. Your girlfriend Milena told us where she was. You may use my first name until you are ready to call me father. My name is Luke by the way." Luke said as he walked out the door.

Luke closed the door. Clicks go off as he locked the door. The wall behind Lily opened. Two muscular men with orange skeleton masks covering their faces walked in the room. They motion for both of them to follow. Luis walked next to Lily.

"What are you going to do about Milena," Lily asked.

"I'm going to kill her," Luis responded.

"Why," Lily asked.

"For being a spy for my father and getting my mother killed. If I'm right she may also be the reason my father sent those shooters to our school." Luis whispered.

"I'm sorry," Lily said.

"Don't be, she chose the wrong person to fuck with," Luis said.

Lily grabbed Luis's hand. She squeezed his hand as he brought it to his lips. He kissed her hand gently before putting it back to his side. They stopped walking before they ran into one of the muscular men. The man stepped aside as Luke walked out of the room they are standing in front of. He smiled at Luis and Lily as he passed by. Luis had the feeling of swinging at his father but ignored it. One of the men looked at Luis.

"You both need to enter now," the man on the right said.

"Why," Luis asked.

"To have your future told by Apollo's oracle. First give me the gun." The man on the right said.

"You can try and take it," Luis said.

"Give it to me now," the man demanded.

"It's empty," Lily said.

"Then you shall pass," the other man said.

"No, he has to prove it," the man on the right said.

The man wanting the gun pushed Lily. Luis caught Lily then made sure she is on her feet. Luis turned to face the man. He eyed the knife on his belt.

"I'll give you a choice. Apologize or die." Luis said in a growl.

"You can't kill me with an empty gun," the man said with a laugh.

"We'll see then," Luis said.

Luis started to swing the gun at the man. He dodged then unsheathed his knife. Lily and the other man watched as Luis made his opponent bleed. Luis knocked him to his knee then broke the man's neck with the gun. To make sure he is dead Luis used the knife to cut the man's throat. Luis looked at the other man.

"You can enter with both weapons," the man said in fear.

"Thank you, kind sir," Luis said.

Luis let Lily enter through the orange curtains with smiling suns on them. Luis walked into a room brightly painted yellow. Orange carpet laid underneath Luis's feet. A blind folded woman sat in a chair with a smile on her face. She moved her hands to remove the blind fold.

"What you are doing is good Luis. These men need to fear you." The woman said.

"Who are you," Lily asked.

"I'm the oracle. Please sit," the oracle said as two chairs appear in front of Luis and Lily.

They take their seats then looked at the women.

"Are you the one who warned my uncle," Luis asked.

"My sister risked her life for you. She used to be the oracle until your father killed her for talking to Jesse. Me and my sister are super-humans like you Luis. She could use fire while I can summon objects. We aren't real oracles like Luke thinks. I make up things because I want one of my lies to kill him. It looks like the lie I have just told him will actually kill him." The oracle said with a smile.

"What is your name," Lily asked.

"My name is Jackie," she said.

"What do you want from me," Luis asked.

"I want you to tell me the story of how you killed your father's men at your school. The story that made you famous." Jackie said as her smile faded.

"Why," Luis asked.

"To know if you can help us escape at any cost," Jackie said.

"Who is us," Lily asked.

"Me, you, her, and the five hundred kidnapped kids," Jackie said sadly.

"I'll do it for the children and Lily," Luis said.

Jackie smiled as Luis reached for Lily's hand. Lily took hold of Luis's hand. Luis started to tell the story of that dreadful day. His words turned into pictures as he described the events to Jackie.

Milena sat at a kitchen table. Jesse sat next to her and watched her stare at Luis's letter. Milena cleared her throat then gave Jesse the letter.

"Can you read this to me? I can't come to read this letter," Milena asked.

"I'd be happy to read it for you," Jesse said.

Milena handed him the letter than drank her coffee. Jesse took the letter then sighed.

"To my dearest Milena. If you are reading this or having Jesse read this to you then I'm not around. I'll return to my normal life one day. Don't wait for me. I want you to find someone else to love. This is good bye. Maybe we'll see each other again."

Jesse gave her the letter with a smile. She smiled and wiped tears from her eyes.

"Jesse I know you trained Luis. I want you to train me like you trained him. Don't try to argue with me to tell me no," Milena said.

"Well I'll train you. Luis may never return to protect you. So, it's good for you to learn to protect yourself." Jesse said with a small smile.

"Thank you, Jesse. Do you think the school will stay open? When do we start?" Milena asked.

"This is the only school we have besides the one being built. The school needs to stay open until the other one is done. We'll start now." Jesse said as he got up from his chair.

Jesse waited for Milena to stand. She stood and followed Jesse into a room with all kinds of weapons on the wall. Milena's eyes widened as she turned looking at the weapons.

"Before we start the real training you must learn the past of Luis. He just found out about his past." Jesse said to Milena.

Luis finished his story then looked at Lily with a hand on her side.

"That next couple of weeks hurt. But we became friends." Lily said with a smile as she looked at their hands.

"Is this the first time you told this story," Jackie asked.

"No, as Lily just said I became friends with her. She asked me what happened to the bodies I was unloading. So, I told her the entire story." Luis said.

"Please wait here," Jackie said as she got up.

Jackie walked to the door. Luis turned around as he heard a little shouting and yelling. Jackie came walking back to her chair. Luis turned back around as she sat down.

"We don't have long but this is how we escape," Jackie said.

"Well how are we going to do this if we aren't trusted," Lily asked.

"Just listen and you'll find out," Jackie said.

"You may continue," Lily said.

"You two will go through seven to eight months of training maybe less or more. You will complete this training and any other missions you are asked to do. After this is done both of you will become the hitmen. Well in Lily's case hit girl. You two will know you are done training when you get all of your weapons and suits. After that you'll have full trust." Jackie said with a smile.

Images of Jackie's next words popped into Luis's head before she spoke. Luis started to smile.

"After we get the trust of my father you can get a truck for the kids to be put in. The building they were put in will be burned to the ground. If we can we'll get another gang leader to help us." Luis said.

"How did you know what I was going to say," Jackie asked.

"I got some gifts of my own," Luis said.

"Sounds good," Lily said.

They all smiled as Luke walked into the room.

"I see you have come to an answer," Luke said.

"Yes, I have," Jackie said.

"What is this answer oracle," Luke asked.

"You will have these two trained. They will be our hit girl and hitman." Jackie said as she stands up.

"Well I'll show them to their room to get some sleep. They'll start training in the morning." Luke said with a smile.

Lily and Luis stand up to follow Luke. After passing a few closed doors Luke slowed down. He started to walk in between Lily and Luis. Luis felt Luke's arm get put around him. Luke started to smile again.

"I remember walking down these halls with your mother. We

were maybe two or three years older than you are now." Luke said with a small smile.

"I don't care about your past," Luis said.

"Well this is your room son," Luke said.

Luke left them in front of the door. Luis and Lily walked into the room. White tile covered the floor. A blue metal bunk bed stood against a green wall. Cabinets, shelves, and lockers cover the other green walls. Lily opened a door to a walk in a closet. Luis opened the other door inside of the closet. That door lead to a bathroom. Luis and Lily let out a sigh as they sat on a bed.

"This is the start of an end," Luis said as Lily put her head on his shoulder.

End of part 2

Part 3

"Do you have the trucks Jackie," Luis asked.

"I do, but Lily is waiting for you," Jackie responded.

"Then I shall go," Luis said.

Luis nodded to Jackie then ran out of her room. He slid to a stop as Lily opened the door with a small box in her hand. Luis followed Lily into the room then shut the door.

"Did you ask her Mr. Black Beard," Lily asked with a smile.

"I know I need to shave. She will have them leave as soon as I give her the word," Luis said.

"You need to get cleaned up," Lily said.

"For what," Luis asked.

Lily rolled her eyes as she put the box in his hands. Luis looked at it to see his name written on it. He looked up to see Lily take her shirt off.

"Why do you take your clothes off in front of me," Luis asked.

"It's fun to have you question me on why I do it. Now get cleaned up." Lily said.

"You never told me what for," Luis said.

"We are to have dinner with Luke in like twenty minutes," Lily said as she took her pants off.

Luis put the box down then stared at Lily while she put on a red dress. He got up and walked toward her. Lily turned to face him. Luis kissed her lips then lifted her up. He walked to the bed with her in his arms. Lily snapped her fingers at Luis.

"Hey, are you still listening to me," Lily asked.

Luis rubbed his eyes.

"Sorry I was thinking of something," Luis said.

"Well stop thinking and open the box," Lily ordered.

"Are you making me," Luis asked with a smile.

"Yes, and stop trying to flirt with me," Lily ordered.

"Hey, I didn't strip in front of you," Luis said.

"Just open the box," Lily said.

"Yes, my loving wife," Luis said.

"You wish I was. You seem a lot happier." Lily said.

"I am because I'm with my best and greatest friend," Luis said.

Luis smiled and winked at her. He opened the box to see a bag of razors and a bottle of shaving cream. Lily walked up to him and looked at the box.

"Thank you, I really needed these," Luis said.

"You are welcome love," Lily said as she gave him a kiss on the cheek.

Luis thought of kissing her but ignored the feeling.

"Only if you knew how I felt," Lily whispered to herself as she walked away.

Luis heard her comment but chose not to respond. He got up and walked toward the bathroom.

"Hey Lily are you ready," Luis asked as he finishes putting on his dress shirt.

"Yes, let's go," Lily said.

Luis opened the door to see his father outside in the hall. Luke smiled as he put his hand on Luis's face. He saw Lily and smiled.

"I see you got him his gifts," Luke said.

"Yes, I have," Lily responded.

"You look great without the beard my son. Are you two ready for dinner?" Luke said with a smile.

"Thank you father and yes," Luis said.

"Then follow me," Luke said.

Luis waited for Lily to close the door. As they walked Luis

grabbed Lily's hand. She looked at their hands then looked away with a small smile. Luke turned to see them holding hands. After a few more turns in the hallway they walked into a dining room. Luke seated himself while Luis pulled a chair out for Lily. After she sat Luis pushed her chair in. Luis sat down with a smile.

"Let's eat before we talk," Luke said.

The waiters in their black and white suits put plates of pizza in front of them. Luis and Lily thanked the waiters then eat. After an hour of silence and eating the table got cleared and gifts are brought to them.

"These two gifts are brought to you but the rest of your gifts are in your room. These are hidden blades with the ability of the knife being able to come out." Luke said with a smile.

Two more waiters brought out two big white bags.

"I had these suits made for the two of you. Now to talk about your mission. You will go to 6023 Rock City road. You two will collect my money from Adan. If he refuses tell him his daughter will no longer breathe." Luke said with a smirk.

"We'll leave now then," Luis said.

Luis grabbed the bags while Lily took the boxes with the hidden blades in them.

"Good luck with your mission," Luke called after them.

They ran to their room in a hurry. After they enter their room Luis looked at the once empty shelves. Guns, knives, bows, crossbows, and other hand to hand combat weapons fill the shelves and cabinets. Luis handed Lily her bag. She took it as she slid his box to him.

"This works perfectly," Luis said.

"What does," Lily asked.

"We can try to convince Adan to help us. If we can tell him we know where his daughter is then he'll help us get her and the others. After that he'll help us kill my father." Luis said with excitement in his voice.

"That could work. After I'm done changing I'll go tell Jackie." Lily said as she took her dress off.

Luis pulled out a red and black trench coat with silver and gold stripes to separate the two colors. Luis smiled as he sees a suit of armor underneath a mask. He pulled out a belt with large pouches and two revolver holsters with a silver dragon symbol on them. On the belt in between the pouches are knife sheathes. He then pulled out the suit of armor and looked at the chest plate. Luis stared at the gold dragon on the chest plate.

"Does your suit come with a mask," Lily asked.

"Yes," Luis said.

Luis turned his head to look at Lily. Lily stood in place with her black and grey armor on. A wolf symbol sat in the middle of her chest. Luis watched as she put the hidden blades on then the trench coat. She looked at the silver covers in the black mask to cover her eyes. Lily sighed then put the mask on.

"You look wonderful," Luis said.

"Don't I always," Lily asked.

"Yes," Luis said.

Luis started to put on his armor as Lily walked out the door. He filled the belt pouches with revolver rounds then put it on. Luis holstered two revolvers then walked to a cabinet. Music went off as Luis opened the cabinet. Luis smiled as his sword with a dragon on the hilt sat in its sheath. He pulled it out and put it on his back. Before Luis answered the video chat that was showing on the television he put his mask on. Luke's face appeared on the screen.

"My son you look exactly how I pictured you would," Luke said.

"Thank you, father. What is it you need?" Luis asked.

"I've called to tell you that you have full access to any motorcycle or car in the garage," Luke said.

Luis put his hidden blades on then put a quiver and bow on his back.

"Thank you, father," Luis said.

"Where is Lily," Luke asked.

"She went to talk to Jackie," Luis said.

"Well then I'll let you go then," Luke said.

Lily walked in as the call ended. She has a phone in her hand. Luis turned toward her.

"Did you get the address," Luis asked.

"Yes, and if we get him to agree she gave me this phone to text her." Lily said as she showed him the phone.

"Before we go I got one stop to make," Luis said.

Lily put the phone away then put the rest of her weapons on. They ran to the garage after Lily and Luis finish getting ready. Two short girls stood guard. They pointed their shotguns at Luis and Lily.

"Do you really want to kill the boss's son," Luis asked.

The girl's eyes widened at his words. They put their weapons away then one opened the door.

"Sorry sir, didn't know," they said as they walked away from the door.

Luis looked around to see two red motorcycles then looked at a car.

"Lily we are taking these two motorcycles," Luis said as he pointed at them.

"Why not take the car," Lily asked.

"Are you scared," Luis asked.

"No," Lily said.

"Then get on one and let's go," Luis said.

Luis got on a motorcycle and turned it on. Lily sighed as she got on the other one.

"Come on love it's going to be fun," Luis said.

Milena climbed out of bed. Jesse walked into her room with a smile.

"You slept in little one. I said if I'm going to train you, you and your mother can stay with me. That also requires you to get up early." Jesse said as he crossed his arms.

"I know but I had to study for my test," Milena said.

"Is that an excuse," Jesse asked.

"I don't know," Milena said.

"Shouldn't you know," Jesse asked.

"Yes," Milena said.

"Good now get up and let's go," Jesse said.

Milena threw up her arms. Jesse laughed as his punches got blocked. Milena and Jesse started throwing punches at each other. They both stopped as Jesse smiled.

"Your training is done but don't stop practicing," Jesse said as he walked out of her room.

Milena smiled then thought of Luis.

"What is this place," Lily asked as they pulled up in front of a grey house.

"My uncle's house," Luis said.

"Why are we here," Lily asked.

"To say hello," Luis said.

"Okay," Lily said.

Luis walked up to the door and knocked. Luis looked at the security camera. He took off his mask and smiled. The door opened with a happy Jesse. Milena stood behind him with a small smile. Mrs. Pool walked forward with a smile. Jesse hugged Luis.

"We have all missed you," Jesse said.

"As have I. Can we come in?" Luis said with a smile.

"Yes," Jesse said.

Luis motioned for Lily to enter before he did himself. Milena and her mom dashed off to the kitchen. Luis looked at Jesse with a smile.

Luis nodded as Jesse passed him and Lily. Lily and Luis stand in the hallway. She faced him after two more seconds.

"Why are we here," Lily asked.

"To see if Milena will admit to working for my father. I also want more information on Adan from Jesse." Luis said.

"Okay, I'm with you till the end," Lily said.

Luis walked up to Jesse. Jesse turned to face Luis.

"I'm about to do something you won't understand. Just trust what I'm about to do." Luis said.

Jesse nodded at Luis then watched him walkover to Lily. She leaned against a wall with her mask off.

"Are you okay," Luis asked.

"What makes you ask that," Lily asked.

"I'm asking you because you look hurt," Luis said.

"It's just that you have a family to return after this and I don't. I'm just an orphan with no parents to love." Lily said with tears in her eyes.

Tears fell from her eyes. She moved her arms to wipe the tears away. Luis pulled her into a hug.

"You can be my family. You are in my heart as much as Desiree is too. Just know I love you and won't stop loving you." Luis whispered in her ear.

More tears fell from her eyes as Lily's warmth filled Luis with happiness.

"I love you and you have no idea how much," Lily said.

"I think I know how much Lily," Luis said.

Milena cleared her throat making Luis and Lily let go off each other. They turned to face Milena holding two cups of tea. Luis took one cup while Lily took the other one. An image of Mrs. Pool and Milena putting a bottle of poison in their tea popped into Luis's head. Luis threw his cup at Milena then slaps the other one out of Lily's hands.

"What are you doing," Lily asked as the tea hit Milena.

"The tea is poisoned Lily. These two poisoned them." Luis growled.

Mrs. Pool came out of the kitchen. Jesse came running from the hall. Luis un-holsters both of his revolvers. He pointed them at Milena and her mother.

"If you wanted to kill me then you should have done better than poison," Luis said.

"Luis, you are being crazy. It's not poisoned. I'd never try to kill the one I love." Milena said.

"Don't fucking move," Luis said.

Mrs. Pool moved.

"Move again and I'll kill you," Luis said.

"You all are crazy we didn't poison the tea," Mrs. Pool said.

Mrs. Pool stepped forward. Luis pulled the trigger then holstered the one aimed at Milena. Tears fell from her eyes as her mother hit the floor.

"You are going to answer all my questions I have for you," Luis said.

More tears stream down her face. Luis put the revolver against her head. Lily saw the anger and hatred in his eyes.

"How long have you been working for my father," Luis asked.

"Since the day I was born," Milena said.

"Pull that chair out and sit in it," Luis ordered.

"No," Milena said.

Luis holsters his revolver then shook his head. He stepped forward then looked back at Lily and Jesse. Luis to turned to face Milena. He put a hand to her face. A tear slowly rolled down her cheek. Luis grabbed hold of her head then slammed it into the table next to her.

"This will go a lot easier if you do what I say. Now pull out that god damn chair." Luis ordered.

Milena pulled out the chair and sat in it.

"Why did my father's people come to our school the day Desiree died," Luis asked.

"I don't know," she said.

Luis released a hidden blade then takes the blade out. He gripped the blade in his hand.

"Why did my father's people come to our school the day Desiree died," he asked again.

"I don't know," she said.

Luis sighed then punched her face. Her head flew backward with a spray of blood and spit shooting out of her mouth. He stabbed the knife through her hand and the chair's arm rest. Milena screamed in pain.

"Answer now," Luis said.

"They came because I asked him to send them to shoot up our school," She said.

"Why," Luis asked.

Milena shook her head no as tears poured down from her eyes. Luis removed the knife from his other hidden blade. He stabbed it through her other hand. Luis unsheathed a knife from his belt. He grabbed her fingers then chopped them off. Luis moved on to the next hand.

"I wanted them to come because I knew I was losing you. I knew that disasters bring couples closer together. That didn't even work because of her. When your father started asking me to spy on you I did. He even wanted your mother dead. I waited until you left the room to call your father after you told me she was leaving to New York." Milena said as she started to cry more.

"You got Desiree and my mother killed because you knew I was going to break up with you. How dare you fuck with my life. How dare you kill the people I loved. How dare you put me in a fight I didn't want to be in." Luis yelled.

"If I didn't do it someone else would have," she said.

Luis sheathed the knife then pulled out the other two. He put the other knives back into his hidden blades.

"Luis I'm sorry. Just know I love you." Milena whimpered.

Anger filled Luis at her words. He started to punch her face repeatedly. Lily tried to step forward to stop him but Jesse stopped her. Blood and teeth start shoot out of her mouth. Luis stopped to catch his breath. He looked at her bruised and puffed up face. Milena bowed her head and spit out blood. Luis wiped the blood off his face then put his mask on. He un-holstered his revolver.

"Luis, I love you," Milena said as she gurgled on her blood.

Luis turned to see a grenade on Lily's belt. Luis holstered his revolver then stepped toward Lily.

"I'm going to need that grenade on your belt," he said.

Lily took it off her belt and gave it to him. Luis walked toward Milena.

"Open your mouth," Luis ordered.

Milena lifted her head to look at Luis. She shook her head no. Luis pulled the grenade's pin then forces it in Milena's mouth.

"Let's go," he said.

They walked down the hall to get away from the blast zone.

"Jesse what can you tell me about Adan," Luis asked.

"I can tell you many things," Jesse asked.

"Can you tell us what you know," Lily asked.

Some of the brain matter from Milena's head flew into the hallway.

"I can do more then tell you. I can take you to him," Jesse said.

"Then suit up because we are leaving now," Luis said.

Jesse nodded then walked down the now dark hallway. Lily looked at Luis.

"What do we do about them," Lily asked.

"We leave them here. My uncle has another house to live in." Luis said as he started walking to the front door.

Lily put her mask on before following Luis. They sat on their motorcycles waiting for Jesse. The garage door opened to show him on a motorcycle in armor. He nodded to them as he drove past them. As they drive off the house exploded. Fire ate the entire house like a bear eating fish. Outside a giant school yard full of buildings with lights on sit Luis and Lily. They turned around to see Jesse running up a path. He bent over to catch his breath.

"What is it Jesse," Luis asked.

"Adan is still at this location. I saw him enter through the gates." Jesse said.

"Then let's go meet him," Luis said.

They all climb onto their motorcycles. Jesse lead the way. Luis thought of his future. A flash of him coming home to three daughters and a wife makes him smile. The day dream faded to him getting married to Lily. Luis shook the dream away as they stopped in front of a silver gate.

"You are in territory not open to the public. State your business or we'll shoot to kill." A man yelled.

Jesse got off his bike and walked up to the gate.

"We are here to speak with your leader Adan," Jesse said.

"Who are you," the man yelled.

"An old friend of the once young night," Jesse said.

A pause made Luis look at Lily then back at the gate. Large lights clicked on showing men and women standing guard. The gate opened as a tall man with light brown hair walked into view. Luis looked at his red pin striped suit. Jesse walked forward with a smile on his face. Luis stared into the man's brown eyes. He watched as the two men hugged each other.

"It is good to see you, old friend," Jesse said.

"It's good to see you too. Who are your two armed kids behind you?" Adan said while looking at Luis and Lily.

"My nephew and his friend Lily," Jesse responded.

"My men will take good care of your nice motorcycles while you talk to me," Adan said.

Three men walked forward. Luis and Lily dismounted the bikes. They watched as the three men walked the motorcycles behind the gate.

"As of until now these three are our guests. Now put your weapons away" Adan told his people.

As they walked behind Jesse and Adan, Luis moved closer to Lily.

"I have to talk to you about something," Luis said.

"We can talk later," Lily responded.

Luis moved away then thought of what he was going to say to Adan. They climbed into an elevator. Adan hit the down button.

"Where we are going," Lily asked

"We are going to my office on the bottom floor. When I bought this place, I had many floors put under the school to hide what I'm doing here." Adan said with a small smile.

"What are you doing here," Luis asked.

"Building an army to kill Luke Hernandez after I get my daughter back," Adan said.

"Then we have a common goal," Luis said.

Adan turned to look at Luis. Luis took his mask off to show his face.

"My name is Luis Hernandez. I'm here to help you so you can help me. I know where your daughter is. I can get her back." Luis said with no emotion.

"If you can do that then me and the other five leaders will help you. Those other five are missing their children too." Adan said sadly.

"Why were they taken," Lily asked.

"When we first go together we tried to kill your father. We lost so he took our children. He told us if we try to fight again he'll kill them." Adan said while looking Jesse.

"He won't because he won't know we are coming," Luis said.

"Luke always knows," Adan said.

"Not when he is fighting a superhuman," Luis responded.

Adan looked at Jesse. Jesse nodded his head. Lily looked at Luis. Adan smiled as the elevator doors opened.

"Get my daughter for me and the others and you'll have an army behind you. Now when do we leave?" Ada said with his smile growing.

"We leave at three in the morning. Make sure the soldiers are ready and well rested." Luis said while stepping out of the elevator.

"Why at three," Adan asked.

"I need to let my person to get the truck there first. She is going to get all the other kids there into the truck and to a police station. These missing kids need to be returned to their parents." Luis said while thinking of Jackie's plan.

"How will you know what kids are ours," Adan asked

"Now that I think of it. My father wouldn't be able to train them as soldiers. He would have them separated from the others. They would be in the heart of the building. These kids will be heavily guarded." Luis said.

"I'll show you to your rooms," Adan said.

"Thank you, Adan," Luis said.

"No, thank you for brining my child back," Adan said.

Luis laid in his bed looking at the galaxy poster on the wall. He got up as someone knocked on the room door. Luis opened the door to see Lily.

"I'm sorry if I woke you up," she said

Before Lily could say another word, Luis kissed her. She let Luis pick her up. He walked backwards after Lily shut the door with her foot. Luis stopped kissing her to catch his breath.

"What are we doing," Luis asked.

"Showing how much we care for each other. Does this mean you care for me Lily?" Luis said with a smile.

Lily kissed Luis again. Luis laid Lily on the bed.

"Are you sure you want this life Lily," Luis asked.

"Stop talking and maybe you'll find out," Lily said.

Luis awakened with Lily curled up next to him with the blanket covering her. He turned his head to look at the clock. Two thirty flashed on the clock. Lily moved making Luis look at her. He kissed her cheek.

"You call that a kiss," Lily said

"How long have you been awake," Luis said.

"Since two. What did you want to talk about?" Lily said with a smile.

"We should have talked first," Luis said.

"Are you saying you didn't like what we just did," Lily asked.

"Not what I'm saying. What we did was fun and great like you." Luis said with a smile.

Lily smiles then Luis kissed her.

"So, what are you saying then," Lily asked.

"Will you be mine? I started to love you since the day I saved you." Luis said.

"I've been in love with you since freshmen year," Lily said.

"Now that I think of it I can't see my life without you. I can't see a life without a part of you in it." Luis said with a smile.

"If you are asking me to be your girlfriend I accept. If you leave me I'll hurt you." Lily said with a little laugh.

"Fair enough," he said.

A phone buzzed on the floor. Lily tried to climb out of bed. Luis held her close to him.

"Where do you think, you are going," Luis asked.

"I'm trying to get the phone," Lily said.

"But once you get up I won't be able to feel the warmth of your soft skin," Luis said.

"If you let me go I promise you'll have me all to yourself," Lily said.

"Now you make me want to just hold you and never let go," Luis said.

"You can never let me go because I can't ever let you go," Lily said.

Luis and Lily stared into each other's eyes. Lily smiled before kissing Luis. He let her go to grab the phone. He stared at the galaxy poster on the wall and thought of the coming battle.

"Luis get up," Lily said.

He sat up to look at her.

"Why," Luis said.

"Jackie has just arrived at the location," Lily said.

Luis jumped out of bed. They rushed to get ready. Luis stood in front of Lily suited up for battle. She gave him one finale kiss before leaving the room. Luis looked at the phone on his bed. He lifted it up then ran out the door. Men and women opened their doors to see Luis running down the hall. He stopped running as he reached Adan's room. Before he could knock on the door it opened. Adan looked at Luis surprised.

"What is wrong," Adan asked.

"She is at the kid's location. We have to move fast," Luis said.

"You give the order. Your soldiers are waiting for your orders," Adan said.

Luis turned to look at the small group of men and women that have gathered.

"It's time for you all to suit up. I understand that you are split up into sections. I want sections A and B to suit up. Sections C through E will pack up this base and move to a new hidden one. Adan will tell you where this location is. When sections A and B are done suiting up for battle report to me. Now move because time is being wasted." Luis ordered.

The hall emptied within seconds. Three leaders walked up to Adan for information. Luis walked to an elevator and hit the button that took him to the main floor. He thought of how to take down the building. The elevator's doors opened and Luis walked out. He slowly turned to see all kinds of different helicopters. Behind the helicopters are armored cars. Adan walked up to Luis in a cloak.

"These are all mine. Well yours now since you are the leader," Adan said.

"How did you get them," Luis asked.

"I bought all of them after I left the special forces," Adan said.

"Is this why your soldiers are trained like soldiers," Luis asked.

"Yes. I also got into to crime so I could help take down the gang leaders. The other five that want your father dead are people I made a deal with. The deal I made with them required them to help me take any other gangster down. If they helped me I would leave them alone and get them a contract with the government. They accepted this deal but made one request." Adan said.

"What was that request," Luis asked.

"If I could train their men like soldiers," Adan responded.

"Why am I the new leader instead of you," Luis asked.

"I'm not young anymore. After the death of your father I'm going to spend all my time raising my child. I'll still be around to help you when you need it though. I can trust you for what you have done and are going to do." Adan said with a smile.

"How did you lose against my father," Luis asked.

Adan let out a sigh.

"He is stronger than any human. He had control over fire," Adan said.

"Humans can kill super-humans if they are working as a single person," Luis said.

"How do you know that," Adan asked.

"I have seen it happen when my mother was killed," Luis said.

"I'm sorry for that. At that time we didn't have that power. We still had leaders giving orders. We had no plan. Now that you are here I believe we can all follow one true leader. As long as you have a plan." Adan said.

"Thank you for believing in me. You are the fourth person that is close to my living family to do so." Luis said thinking of Lily, Desiree, and Jackie.

"No problem but it's time to tell us your plan," Adan said.

Luis turned to face the soldiers in the room. Lily and Jesse stood looking at Luis. Adan joined the long ranks of battle ready soldiers.

"The way this will work is for us to fight together. One of us falls and meets death today keeping moving. Fight harder for each person that falls today or has fallen. None of you are just thugs. Each and every one of you is perfect in your own way. I look at you as my new family to grow close to. I look at you as my family of soldiers. Section A will be the ground team. You will be the ones attacking from the ground. You will be the enemies primary focus. You will take the heavily armored vehicles. Jesse and Adan are your commanders. Section B will be taking the helicopters. You will be going into that building and getting the kids out. Lily and I will be with you. We will be in contact with each other with the walkie-talkies on that wall. Section A you are free to leave after you take one. Section B get one too. I'll see all of you on the other side." Luis said.

The soldiers shouted in approval then burst into action. Jesse and

Adan winked at Luis. Adan walked off as Jesse walked up to Luis. Luis put on his mask.

"Your mother would be proud," Jesse said.

"Thank you. Jesse after Jackie starts to leave I want some soldiers to go guard the truck while until they reach a police station," Luis said.

"It will be done and good luck," Jesse said.

"Good luck to you father," Luis said.

Jesse's eyes watered as he ran off. Luis climbed into a helicopter after Lily handed him a walkie talkie. The quiet night sky started to awaken. Luis looked out the window. He thought of Desiree dying in his arms. The memory of her cold body against his warm body made him shiver. Luis came back to the present as Lily put a hand on his arm.

"Luis we are attacking. There are some men on the roof. We can't push forward until they are dead," Adan said.

"Copy that Adan, they will be taken care of," Luis said.

Luis turned to the soldiers in his helicopter.

"Section B open your doors and fire on the enemy forces on the ground and roof top," Luis ordered.

Luis felt the wind as the doors slid open. He took his bow off his back. He nocked an arrow as the others opened fire. The other helicopters followed his action. Men started to fall to the floor as death rushed across the battlefield. Luis watched as blood shot out of the men's necks on the giant square building underneath them. Section A started to push forward. Luis put his bow back on his back then walked to the pilot's chair.

"Take us down so we can enter the building. After we are all out return home to help clean up," Luis said.

"Yes sir," the pilot responded.

The helicopter slowly lowered. Luis looked outside to see a man running across the roof. Luis unsheathed his sword then jumped out of the helicopter. Lily screamed out his name. Luis stabbed his sword through a man's head. A door slammed open. Luis turned to see a new group of men running out of a dark staircase. He ran at the men with his sword ready to strike.

"It's the dragon, he has come to save us," one of them men said.

The men scream as Luis started to slice off their limbs. Blood splattered across the roof as he stabbed the men. Luis picked a grenade off one of their belts. He pulled the pin then threw it down the staircase. Another door slammed open. Women rushed out of that one with guns raised. Luis kicked the door closed then picked up a dead body. He used it as a shield as he ran toward the women.

"You are a traitor," one of them yelled.

"No, I'm just your nightmare being unleashed," Luis said.

Luis threw his sword. The women shot backward with the sword sticking through her jaw. He threw the body then un-holstered his revolvers. Each step he took he fired off a round. The women ran to cover behind a couple of air vents. Luis holstered his revolvers as soon as they emptied. He released his hidden blades as he sprinted at the girls. They jumped up to take shots at Luis.

"Stop or die," they yelled.

"You'll be the one to die," Luis said.

Luis jumped over the air vent kicking a girl off the roof. Another girl pulled out a knife. She jumped at Luis. He blocked her attack. She screamed out in pain as Luis broke her arm. He retracted the blades then broke her neck. Luis threw her off the roof. He picked the knife off the floor. The door slammed open again. Luis threw the knife at the women in the doorway. As Luis grabbed his sword he looked around to see twenty dead bodies. The soldiers looked around to see Luis's work. The soldiers on the helicopter opened fire on the other soldiers coming out of the door. When the gunfire stopped, the soldiers stepped off the helicopter.

"He is like a ghost. They couldn't even touch him," one of the soldiers said.

Lily is the last one to get on the roof. Luis cleans the blood off his sword then sheaths it. He reloads both of his revolvers then looks at forty soldiers in front of him.

"There are two entrances to the building from here. We will split up into two groups of twenty. I'll lead one group while Lily leads the other group."

They split up into groups. Luis looked over at Lily then nodded. Luis kicked open the door. Lights started to flicker in the staircase. They stopped moving as they reached a door. Luis put his head against the door.

"Sir we have some of the children in this room. We have four of the children. The other three are in the basement." A soldier said inside the room.

"You can't move them outside. We are losing to much ground. Stay put," Someone responded.

Luis backed away from the door. He looked at the soldiers waiting for orders.

"Five of you are going to stay with me. The rest of you are going to the basement. There are three kids down there. Once you have them get to the roof. You five are going to stay out here while I get the kids inside." Luis said.

Five soldiers stepped aside as the others rushed down the stairs. Luis quietly opened the door. A girl with blonde hair looked at him. He put a finger to his face telling her to stay quiet. She nodded then laid on the floor. The other kids laid on the floor. Five men walked around the room. The building started to shake making the lights turn off. Luis rushed into the room and took cover behind a desk. Flashlights turned on in the room as the lights turned off.

"Looks like they cut the power," one of the soldiers said.

One of the men threw a flare onto the middle of the floor. Luis dodged one of the men's flashlight beam. The flare's light got blocked by a kid. Luis released a hidden blade. He waited for a man to pass by him. Luis covered the man's mouth then slit his throat. He retracted the blade then slowly put him on the floor. Luis grabbed the assault rifle as the flare went out.

"Someone put another one down," soldier said.

Another man lights a flare. He saw Luis standing with the gun aimed at him. Luis opened fire on the man then shot the other four. The bodies hit the floor as Luis crouched down.

"You kids are all safe now. I'm going to take you to your parents. Just follow me." Luis said.

They all got up and followed Luis. He opened the door to the stair case. The soldiers looked to see Luis standing next to the kids.

"What now sir," a soldier asked.

"We get to the roof. Contact Lily and tell her to get to the roof. I also want a chopper called in." Luis said while he looked at the children.

The soldiers nodded as Luis walked past them. Two soldiers got on their walkie-talkies. After they finished they started to run up the stairs. Luis kicked open the door then put a hand up to cover his eyes. He blocked the sun from his view. Footsteps started to echo in the hallway.

"Get behind me kids," Luis said.

Luis raised his gun as the other soldiers aimed at the door.

"You'll die if you step onto this roof," Luis said.

"It's us sir. We need to hurry. Luke's troops are coming up to the stairs." A soldier said from the staircase.

"Let them pass," Luis said.

Luis watched as three kids walked out of the dark staircase. Behind them are five women.

"Where is the rest," Luis asked.

"They stayed behind to cover our escape," one of them said.

"Let's hope Lily gets up here or the choppers get to us," Luis said.

Luis handed a soldier his assault rifle.

"Are the kids there," Adan asked over the walkie-talkie.

"Yes, I'm here with them. What is it you need?" Luis responded.

"We have taken the battlefield," Adan said.

"Are there any kind of explosives with you," Luis asked.

"Yes, there are. Do you have my daughter?" Adan said.

"Yes I do. Set those explosives on the building and set them off when I give the order." Luis ordered.

"It will be done and thank you," Adan said.

Luis turned to see the helicopters come into sight. He took his bow off his back. The other door slammed open. A man came running out with Lily chasing after him. Luis nocked an arrow then aimed at the man. He released the arrow. The arrow went through the man's leg making him fall to the floor. Lily un-holstered her pistol and shot the man. Twenty men and women came running behind her. Helicopters hovered next to the building.

"Help get the kids on first," Luis said.

Luis and Lily watched the doors the as the kids got put on the chopper. The chopper flew off as men started coming through the stair well. Luis started shooting them down with arrows. After he ran out of arrows he put his bow on his back. Lily unsheathed her sword then ran forward. Luis did the same with a smile. Luis and Lily stood side by side covered in blood. Luis threw his sword at a man. They turned to get on the helicopter.

"Adan blow the building," Luis said as they flew off.

Luis held Lily in his arms as they watched the building start to crash. The helicopter's doors closed. Luis fell asleep while holding Lily. Lily put her head on his shoulder.

"Milena was right about tragic events bringing loved ones together," Lily said to herself.

Lily looked at Luis as he stood in front of a camera. She then looked at the kids next to her.

"My name is Luis Hernandez. This is my girlfriend Lily Sky Griffin. These are your kids we have saved from my father. Adan has made me leader of his gang. I don't want you to make me leader of your gangs. All I want is for you to be an ally to the Broken army. Please help me bring an end to my father. If you join you will no longer be gangsters but heroes and soldiers. If you don't join please come get your children. They miss their parents deeply. Thank you for your time." Luis said as he aimed the camera at Lily and the kids.

Luis stopped the tape. He put the address underneath the video in the email then sent it. Luis walked to the kids then got on one knee.

"Hey guys, I just emailed your parents. They should be here today or tomorrow," he said with a smile.

Adan walked into the room with Jesse and a woman behind him. Luis stood up and shook Adan's hand.

"Alright kids it's time for lunch and a movie," the woman said.

The kids smiled as they followed the woman out of the room. After the room door closed Luis turned to Adan and Jesse.

"Did you email them," Jesse asked.

"Yes," Luis said.

"Okay well I want to know your plan for killing your father," Adan said.

"If I know him well then I know what he is going to do. He is going to take everybody and everything I love." Luis said while he glanced over to Lily.

"What are those things," Adan asked.

"What I love most is Lily, Cardinal High, and my uncle," Luis said.

A chime went off from the computer. Jesse turned to the computer. Luis saw the emails open. Jesse turned back around then smiled.

"All the other leaders are in. They have two requests." Jesse said.

"What are the requests," Luis asked.

"You lead their people as you lead Adan's people. They also want complete protection for their kids." Jesse said with a smile.

Luis paced for a couple of seconds then looked at Adan.

"Do you have any more secret places to hide," Luis asked.

"I have a house with an underground bunker. What do you need it for?" Adan responded.

"After they see their children I want the kids moved to that house. That means your kid too." Luis said.

"Who will protect them," Lily asked.

"Jesse and the other hitmen will. When will they be here?" Luis said.

"Two are an hour away the others are six hours away," Adan said.

"Good, very good. I want all of my soldiers not taking care of those children cleaning and making room for the rest of our soldiers." Luis said.

"What will you do," Adan asked.

"Me and Lily will plan on how to protect the school when it's attacked," Luis answered.

Adan and Jesse walked out of the room. Luis dropped to his knees as some images rushed into his head. Lily jumped to her feet. Luis put out a hand for het to stay where she was. Luis opened his eyes. The room changed to a dark room with a single light that dangled from the ceiling. A tall girl in black armor with the letters S.H. in the middle of her chest stepped forward. She moved closer to Luis. A dark black hood covered her face.

"Who killed my husband Eric," the women asked.

"The famous hero who saved his school and your sister's school," someone said behind her.

"You may leave now so I can finish my work here with Thomas," the women said.

A door opened and slammed closed behind the women. Luis felt the punch the women gave Thomas.

"Whatever you want to know about Power Tree is something you will never get," Thomas said.

"Why is that," the women asked.

"I am from the intelligence branch of the Power Tree army. No matter what torture you put me through you will never get the answers you seek." Thomas said.

Luis started to hear a voice in his head say, "I'll find a way to talk to you later just know there are more superhumans like you in this world. I am Thomas."

The scene he just saw disappeared as he closed his eyes again. Luis opened his eyes to see Lily crouched next to him.

"What is wrong," she asked.

"You know how I said I was a superhuman," Luis said.

"Yes, I do but what does that mean," Lily asked.

"Well the army my mom was working with have superhumans like me and other superhumans not like me. I just saw, felt heard, and smelled, what a superhuman named Thomas was going through." Luis said as he got to his feet.

"Are you okay," Lily asked.

"I'm fine it's just that each time something like this happens my mind feels stronger. The only thing for right now is I don't know how to use my gift. Maybe if we meet another superhuman like me I can learn to control my gifts." Luis said.

"Have you used your gift before," Lily asked.

"I have used it before. The first time was in the school gym when I was holding Desiree in my arms. The second time was when I was fighting Owl and I knocked over the burning tree. The third time was when Jackie's other half of her plan popped into my head. The last time besides now was when I had an image of Milena and her mother putting poison in our tea." Luis said while thinking of all the events.

"I'm guessing your gift helps you when you need it most. Until you learn how to use it all the time we won't know when it will help you until it happens." Lily said as she stood up.

"You ready to start planning," Luis asked.

"Yes, I am," Lily responded.

After ten hours of cleaning and planning have past all the soldiers were ordered to stand in a great hall. They stood waiting for the meeting to begin. Luis walked up to the old six leaders that stood on the stage. Adan stepped forward.

"We thank you for saving our children. We also want to wish you good luck. Now let us all hear your plan." Adan said with a smile.

"I'd like to let you know that you six are captains as well," Luis said.

The six captains bowed to Luis. He walked over to Lily. Luis looked at the soldiers under his command. He took a deep breath before speaking.

"All of you are going through changes you don't understand. Each and every one of you are now under my command. Yes, I'm a teenager but those of you who fought with me know what we are able to do. My father has done so much damage to all of you. You are all going to have a hand in killing my father. If you don't want to fight you have the choice to leave. You may leave now." Luis said.

Luis watched as they talked amongst themselves. Lily put a hand on his shoulder. She whispered in his ear.

"I've just got an email from Jackie. Your father has just filmed a video. She said it's all over the internet." Lily said.

"Put it on the big screen," Luis said.

Lily nodded as she walked away. The talking stopped as Luis faced a giant screen behind him on the wall. Luke's face appeared on the screen. Behind him is a destroyed building. Luke put a hand to his face.

"You have no idea how much it pains me to see my soldiers killed and my property taken. My son is the one who did this. Those of you who know my son will not be happy. He has an army to back him up. That army will protect him and him alone. I need to apologize to all of you. Cardinal High will be attacked. I'm attacking this school again because my son loves this school. He took my daughter that I loved so much. I loved her more than my two sons. I also need to thank my son for getting rid of his brother. If he didn't I was going to have him killed. Cardinal High just know you will never stand again. Luis Hernandez I'm coming for you." Luke said.

Luke removed his hand from his face as the video ended. Luis turned to look at the soldiers.

"This video was made to scare you. It was made to show his power. I'm not afraid of him and nor should you. He is coming after that school because I have freed five hundred children he stole and had locked in that building. Now that you have made your choice here is our plan." Luis said.

The screen changed to a map of a school with houses circled in red.

"Each of you will be at one of those houses surrounding Cardinal High. Lily and I will go back to school as students. You will wait till my school is attacked by my father. After he attacks that's when you will move in to fight. My father's forces out number us but we have the advantage. We have the advantage because we can surprise them. We also know the school grounds more than they do. We have a fighting chance. We will win this fight because we don't fear anyone. My father's forces will learn to fear us." Luis said with excitement.

The soldiers shouted in approval then quieted down.

"Each of you to will report to your captains. Your captains have the address of where you are stationed. All the hitmen out there will report to captain Jesse Williams for your orders. Welcome to the Broken army my soldiers." Luis said.

Luis pointed to the six captains to his left before he walked off stage. Lily walked up to Luis then looked at Jesse. Jesse stepped in front of Luis and Lily.

"Your mother would be proud," Jesses said.

"Thank you, my father," Luis said.

Jesse's eyes started to water. Lily smiled as Luis hugged Jesse.

"You are my father more than Luke is. I'm glad to share blood with you. To help you out I have sent thirty soldiers to the house right now. Good luck captain." Luis said.

"Good luck to you my son," Jesse said.

Luis let him go. Jesse wiped his eyes as he walked to the hitmen waiting for him. Luis turned to face Lily. He gave her a kiss. After he kissed her he got on one knee. Luis pulled out folded up piece of paper.

"Lily Sky Griffin I know we just started dating but I can't date you. The day I saved from that villain Swords Master I knew I loved you. I didn't want to admit it even when we became friends. The more I spent time with you the more I fell madly in love with you. I can't live in a world without you by my side. Will you go to prom with me?" Luis said as he unfolded the paper.

Lily looked at the paper that said prom with a question mark.

"Only if you promise to never stop loving me," Lily said.

"I promise with all my heart," Luis said.

He stands up then gave her a kiss. They held hands as they walked down the hallway.

"Yay, we get to study for test again," Lily said.

"Well at least we get to be normal teens for a while love," Luis said.

A month passed after Luis and Lilly have gone back to Cardinal High. Each day Luis wrote in a notebook with the title "Broken Hero" on the front cover.

"Why aren't you getting dressed," Lily asked.

"I don't have to," Luis said.

"Yes, you do. Our prom is tonight. You are such an ass sometimes." Lily said.

"What did I do," Luis asked with a smile.

"You are acting like you forgot tonight," Lily said.

"Why is our prom at the school again," Luis asked.

"The school didn't have enough money to put it in a fancy hotel because they had to fix the school twice," Lily said.

Luis blocked her from going to the bathroom. He gave her a kiss. She pushed him to the side.

"Get dressed," Lily said with a laugh.

Luis smiled as he put on a dark red and black suit. Lily walked out of the bathroom in a maroon dress. Luis stood there staring at her.

"You look as wonderful as the night stars," Luis said.

Lily smiled as she fixed the ring Luis gave her. As they walked down stairs Adan pulled out a camera. Flashes go off as Adan went crazy with taking pictures. Luis tried to take the camera from Adan.

"Hey Jesse, is going to want pictures," Adan said.

"Not this much," Lily and Luis said.

"Oh, hush you two," Adan said.

Adan smiled then put the camera down. He let the happy couple pass. Adan waved good bye to them as they walked up the street.

"I shouldn't have put heels on," Lily said.

"Why," Luis said.

"If there is no attack I'll have to walk there, dance and walk back in these heels. You wouldn't understand how much heels hurt." Lily said.

"I do understand because I used to be in ballroom. Guys feet would hurt if they were not used to the dance shoes." Luis said.

"Oh, I forgot about that," Lily said.

Luis stopped walking and pulled Lily aside. He pulled her into a kiss but kept his eyes open. A strange man in all black stood across the street. A car passed by and the light reflected on something shiny. The man walked away after a few more seconds. Luis stopped kissing Lily.

"When we get into the school we need to call our friends. It might happen tonight." Luis said.

"So much for this night," Lily said.

Luis winked at Lily then picked her up. She put her arms around his neck. Lily laughed as he walked with her in his arms.

"I love the ride to the dance but why," Lily asked.

"Your feet won't be killing you all night," Luis said with a smile.

"Thank you, my one true love," Lily said.

Luis put Lily down as they stood in rose petals. White lights ran along the path leading to the main gym. As they walked into the gym flashes of Desiree dying in Luis's arms came back to him. Luis put a hand to his head and shook his head. Lily looked at Luis.

"Are you okay," Lily asked.

"I keep remembering Desiree. I'll be fine. Let's go make that call." Luis said with a weak smile.

Luis led Lily off somewhere quiet. The song changed to a slow song as Adan's face appeared on Lily's phone.

"What is wrong," Adan asked.

"Get the men ready for a fight. My father might attack to night. Once you hear gunfire don't hesitate to come. Bring our armor with you. You'll find us in the main gym." Luis said.

"How do you know," Adan asked.

"I have seen one of my father's spies outside the school," Luis responded.

"What about the other students," Adan asked.

"We'll get them out," Lily said.

"We'll be ready," Adan said.

Luis ended the call then led Lily to the dance floor. Lily looked at him with a confused look.

"What are we doing," Lily asked.

"We are going to dance in a circle until we spot the principal," Luis said.

"You know I only could sneak in one knife," Lily said.

"When we start to fight my father's forces I'll get a weapon," Luis said.

"I just want you to live to see another day," Lily said.

"I will because I promised you that," Luis said.

Lily smiled as Luis looked for the principal. The song ended as the principal stepped on stage. Lily leaned close to Luis.

"I found him," Lily said.

Luis turned to see him on the stage. He sighed as the music stopped.

"I know the music is great but you get to find out who the prom king and queen are," the principal said.

The students clapped. The principal pulled a card out of his jacket pocket.

"Your prom king and queen is Luis Hernandez and Lily Griffin. Please come onto the stage." The principal said with a smile.

They walked onto the stage. A teacher put a crown on Luis and Lily's head. The principal handed Luis the microphone. Luis smiled at the principle.

"Students and staff at Cardinal High I have very important news for you. This prom must end now. That video warning my father put on the internet wasn't a lie. He is going to attack this school now. All of you take the back exit and leave. Me and Lily will take care of the school, now go." Luis ordered.

The building shook scaring students. The lights dimmed as the building stopped shaking. Luis looked at the lights as they turned on again. Lily looked at Luis then pulled a knife from under her dress.

"There is no time now go," Luis said.

The teachers ran to the back of the gym. Students followed the teachers as they unlocked the doors. Luis and Lily took the crowns off their heads. They ran to the doors. Luis poked his head out the door. Soldiers started running to the gym's lobby. Luis closed the doors as they started shooting at the door. He looked back at Lily.

"How many are there," Lily asked.

"It looks like twenty or thirty soldiers. They have AK-47's and swords. All we need to do is hide next to the doors. They will enter and that's when we'll strike." Luis said.

Lily nodded as she put her back against the brick wall. Luis felt his heart pounding in his chest. Seconds ticked by as the soldiers walked into the gym. Luis slammed the door closed on a soldier. Lily stabbed one in the throat as Luis snapped one's neck. He picked the two guns up from the floor. Lily took one from him. The doors burst open. Luis and Lily walked backwards as they fired at the soldiers. Body after body hits the floor. The last five soldiers unsheathed their swords then ran at Luis and Lily. Luis dodged a swing and felt a sharp pain on his arm. He put a hand to his left arm. Warm blood touched his fingers. Luis looked at the man who cut him.

"I liked this suit," Luis said.

Luis dodged a swing then hit him with the gun's butt. He continued to hit the man. Blood ran down from the man's eye and nose. Lily broke a women's arm to disarm her. The sword clattered to the floor. Lily kicked it to Luis. Luis kicked the man backwards then picked up the sword. He gripped the sword tighter as a girl screamed inside his head. He shut his eyes and let out a scream. The soldiers looked at Luis as he chopped off a man's head. He ran to them with his eyes shut. They all attacked him. Fear built inside of the soldiers as they dropped like flies. The last soldier backed away slowly. Luis opened his eyes.

"I've got questions for you. They are very easy. The first one is kind of funny. Do you know the muffin man?" Luis said with a laugh.

"I don't talk to monsters," the soldier said.

Luis laughed a little more.

"Don't you know? I'm Luke's son. I'm the one he calls the dragon." Luis said.

"That's why you are the monster," the soldier said.

The door behind the scared man opened. Adan ran in with his assault rifle aimed at the man. He pulled the trigger. As the man hit the floor Adan whistled.

"You two need to get dressed fast," Adan said.

"Why," Luis asked.

"The battle has just started," Adan responded.

A man and women came into the gym with a backpack in their arms. Luis and Lily ran up to take the bags.

"All of your weapons are in the backpacks except for your swords," Adan said.

Another woman ran inside the gym with a bow and quiver on her back. Gunfire went off outside. Luis thanked all four of them as he grabbed his bow and quiver. Luis and Lily ran to the nearest bathroom. Adan ordered the others to pick up the guns and ammo off the dead bodies.

"Are you okay Luis," Lily asked.

"I'm fine Lily," Luis said.

"You don't seem fine," Lily said.

"Why do you say that," Luis asked.

"You started to act insane," Lily said.

"I only did that because I can't get her death out of my head.

Maybe when he is dead I won't remember that part anymore." Luis said.

"Find a way past this and I'll be fine with whatever you do," Lily said.

Luis stood in front of the bathroom sink looking at himself in the mirror. He looked at the silver eyes staring back at him. The girl started to scream in his head again.

"Who is screaming in my head," he asked himself.

Luis started to think of Desiree, Milena, and Lily. A guy with short brown hair and brown eyes appeared in the mirror. Blood ran down the side of his head.

"Who are you," Luis asked.

"I don't have much time to explain everything. Me and my wife are being hunted. I only have time for me to talk to you. Just listen then I'll give you a full introduction before I leave." The man said.

Luis nodded at the strange man.

"I'm a superhuman like you. We are part of the same branch to the power tree. I'm talking to you by using my mind. The girl screaming in your head is my wife. We can hear through each other's ears by having a mind link. I am pretty sure you turned the link on." The man said.

Something crashed making the man turn.

"You are just discovering the great power we have. That is a good thing. Using the abilities are just like working out a muscle at the gym. My name is Thomas and me, my wife Emma or our friend Julia will find you. Right now, you get only one question." Thomas said.

"How am I able to see you," Luis asked.

"You can see me through the mind link. It's just like having a conversation with the person in front of you or having a chat on a face time call. The only difference is only people part of the mind branch can activate it. We can also taste, see, hear, feel, and read each other's thoughts if we have a mind link between each other. I'm sorry but I need to go now I promise you will be found and trained more once I'm not being hunted. Here is the story of me and Emma and hopefully a better explanation." Thomas said.

Images rushed through Luis head as he felt Thomas's presence leave his mind. Everything went dark as Luis lived through Thomas's memory.

End of part 3

Part 4

A man with short brown hair and brown eyes looked around the room. The man looked down at himself as a woman with blue eyes and black hair sat down next to him. The woman was dressed in blue and black elvish battle armor. The woman looked at the man with a smile on her face.

"Thomas, are you ready to learn," the woman said.

"Yes, but who is going to teach us Emma," Thomas asked.

Emma shrugged as the door to the small square room opened. A tall woman will long blonde hair walked into the room. Her green eyes light up as she looked at Emma and Thomas. Thomas looked at her red and black elvish battle armor. A symbol of fire sat in the middle of her chest.

"Captain Julia Rubussay how are you friend," Thomas said playfully.

"You don't have to call me that," Julia said.

"But we just got used to saying that," Emma said.

"Well since you two have been promoted to captain you don't have to call me that," Julia said.

"How did we get promoted to captain if it takes more than three years to get the rank captain if we want that rank, Thomas asked.

"During the battle against Collin in the city Vision the queen heard about you two. She learned during that battle both of you learned how to master your abilities in the branches you belong to. She also heard of how you took on her brother Extremo Oscuro. For

81

both of you defeating him and gaining us the territory promoted you to captains. We don't know if he is killed but we do know that you have injured him." Julia said.

Julia turned to the white wall behind her. She took her glove off and put her hand on the wall. Thomas watched as the wall split apart and a giant white flat screen appeared. The ceiling above Emma and Thomas opened so a projector could come out. The projector turned on and the white screen turned blue. Someone knocked on the door. Julia moved to open the door. A tall shiny metal man with gold eyes stood in the door way with battle armor in his arms.

"Captain Julia I have Captain Emma's and Thomas's proper battle armor." The metal man said.

"Thank you Jyn," Julia said as she took the armor.

"You are welcome Captain," Jyn said.

Julia closed the door then handed Thomas a suit of black and purple elvish battle armor with an owl in the middle of the chest plate. Julia handed Emma a suit of black and blue elvish battle armor. In the middle of the chest plate is a symbol of a rain drop.

"These are the suits of armor we already have on except for the symbol," Thomas said.

"Soldiers that are not captains or higher ranking officers only get armor with the branches colors that they belong to. Those that are not superhumans get armor with a different colored tree in the middle of their chest and shoulders." Julia said.

"That makes a little more sense," Thomas said.

Julia smiled then put her glove back on. Thomas watched as Julia pulled a clicker out of her belt pocket. Julia pressed a button on the clicker. The screen changed to a slide with the words welcome to power tree on it in bright white letters. The slide changed to a symbol of a purple and black owl.

"This owl is the symbol of the intelligence branch. The Intelligence branch is the branch you belong to. Their colors are purple and black. The Intelligence branch deals with superhumans that can do things with their minds." Julia said as she changed the slide.

A symbol of a black and blue rain drop appeared. Emma smiled as she looked down at her armor.

"This is the symbol of the water branch. The water branch deals with superhumans that can control any type of water. That means they can also freeze the water they summon or suck the water out of an organism. The colors are blue and black." Julia said.

The slide changed to a symbol of fire with the colors red and black.

"This is the branch I am from. The fire branch ability is allowing a superhuman to control fire and be able to turn it into any type of weapon." Julia said.

"Are you just telling us the basics of each branch," Thomas asked as she changed the slide.

Julia nodded as the symbol of a small man appeared in an orange and black suit.

"This is the size branch. They can shrink down in height or grow. These superhumans can also grow in width. The next branch is called animal." Julia said as the slide changed.

A symbol of a bear in yellow and black elvish battle armor appeared on the screen.

"The animal branch allows the superhuman to change in any kind of animal that is alive or dead." Julia said.

The slide changed to a symbol of green arm holding a black rock.

"This is the earth branch. The earth branch can control anything that came from any of the planets they are on. They also have super strength." Julia said with a smile.

The slide changed as a symbol of a bird wing popped up.

"This is the flight branch. Each superhuman from this branch can grow bird wings. They can also control the weather. These superhumans also have super speed. Their colors are grey and black." Julia said.

"Is that all the branches," Emma asked.

Julia changed the slide to black screen with the letters S.H. in red. Thomas looked at the symbol then at Emma.

"Colin had mentioned them," Thomas said.

"This is a small enemy army called the Superhuman Hunters. They go by S.H. as well as Superhuman Hunters. We don't know why they hate superhumans but we believe they are working with Extremo Oscuro. Extremo Oscuro has his army of evil monsters that has lived on this earth before the man and elves. Now we have two armies trying to hunt us down." Julia said with a frown.

"Has there ever been a superhuman that is able to control every ability from each branch," Emma and Thomas asked.

"There were two but after they had their kids Extremo Oscuro killed his niece and nephew," Julia said.

"So those two superhumans were the queen's children," Thomas asked.

"Yes, and they were the first superhumans," Julia said.

Julia changed the slide one last time. A giant golden brown raccoon paw print appeared on the white slide. Thomas looked at it with wonder.

"This is your mission. This is the symbol to the Creator's army. The queen was allies with the Creator. The Creator has an army of animals that can talk in any language and have the same gifts as the superhumans. We call them super-animals. They are classified in the tree just like we are. We need his help now more than ever. The queen wants you two to go out and find and convince him to join our side." Julia said with a hopeful smile.

"It will be done if me and Emma can get married first," Thomas said.

"That can be done," Julia said.

Julia turned everything off as they all walked out of the room.

"Let's go get you two hitched," Julia said with a hug smile.

"I like the sound of that," Emma said while she held Thomas's hand.

The end of part 4

Part 5

Thomas got replaced with Luis's reflection when he opened his eyes. Lily stepped out of the bathroom stall dressed in her armor. Luis pushed what he found out to the back of his mind. He looked at Lily.

"Are you ready," he asked.

"Ready as I'll ever be," she said.

Luis took his bow off his back as Lily ran out the door. As they stepped outside something exploded into flames. Adan ran out of a building. Luis started shooting arrows at the enemy soldiers following him.

"We pushed them back to the middle of the school," Adan said.

"That's good," Luis said.

"We are going to lose unless we stop them from running out of that building," Adan said.

Luis looked to see Adan pointing at a brown building with a one hundred on it.

"Get me a small group of soldiers. Me and Lily will clear out that building. You and the other captains keep pushing them back. Attack from all sides if you can." Luis ordered.

Adan nodded as he made a motion to a group of soldiers reloading their guns. They finished and ran over to Luis and Lily.

"What do you need sir," the soldiers asked.

"You six will come with us. We will clear out any enemy in that building." Luis said.

Adan smiled as he ran off. Luis knocked an arrow as a soldier poked his head out the door. He aimed at the soldier and waited. The door opened all the way as Luis released the arrow. Lily watched as the glass door started to crack at the impact of the soldier's dead body.

"Let's move," Luis said.

They ran forward as a grenade soared through the air. Luis slid to a stop pulling Lily aside. The other soldiers followed them to take cover. They hid in the boy's bathroom. The entire ground shook as bricks came loose and scattered across the floor outside. Lily stuck her head outside.

"It's clear of grenades," Lily said.

"Then we better run like hell," Luis said.

They all got up and run to the one hundred building. Luis crossed his arms as he jumped through a window. He rolled over a table behind a bookshelf. The others jumped through the same window. Luis drew an arrow as he watched a guard walk across the library. The soldier dropped to the floor with a small gasp. Lily pulled two knives from her belt. Two more soldiers walked into view. She threw the knives then watched blood splatter from their throats. Luis took his quiver off his back.

"You couldn't go through the front door," Lily asked.

"Where is the fun in that? Well I got two arrows left." Luis said.

Luis stood up holding the two arrows in his hand. He walked up to the soldier with an arrow sticking out of her throat. Blood started to darken the carpet as her eyes lay open. Luis shook his head as Lily walked up to him.

"She looks like she is fourteen," Luis said.

"That's your father. He turns young children into soldiers that start to fight once they are kidnapped." Lily said.

"That is why he is going to die," Luis said.

Luis opened the library door. He looked left and right to see the hallway empty. Lily stepped behind Luis looking down at the right hallway. The soldiers looked left.

"You six go down the right hallway while we go down the left," Luis said.

"Yes sir," the soldiers replied.

Luis knocked both arrows as footsteps started to pound down the hallways.

"Stand your ground," Lily yelled.

Soldiers stopped running as they saw Luis aiming at them. He released both arrows then unsheathed his new sword. Lily did the same as Luis ran forward. Behind them gunfire went off as metal collided with metal. Each swing from Luis and Lily created blood splatter. They stood side by side panting like dogs.

"How many of them are there," Lily asked.

"Let's just say a lot of people need to be killed. Get ready for some more Lily." Luis said.

Luis un-holstered his revolver. Weapon less soldiers came running down the hall. Luis shot two of them then holstered his weapon. Luis grabbed a scared soldier as Lily stabbed the other one.

"Why are you running," Luis asked.

"We are running from the dogs," the soldier said.

"What dogs," Lily asked.

"The dogs the other army brought," the soldier replied.

A German Shepard came running down the hallway. Luis threw the soldier to the floor. He watched as the dog ripped out the soldier's throat.

"Men stand down," Luis said.

A girl with cherry red hair walked down the hall. Luis looked at her black armor. The letters S.H. sat in the middle of her chest. Luis looked at the other soldiers in the same black armor and had the same letters on their chests. Black helmets covered their faces. The girl's blue eyes stared down Luis. Luis pointed his sword at the girl.

"Who are you," Luis asked.

"I'm your sister-in-law. My name is Cassie Hernandez. These soldiers are my Superhuman Hunters. I am their leader." Cassie said.

"Why are you here," Luis asked.

"I still hate you for killing my husband. I hate your father more. We are going to help you just this once. We hunt down super-humans and kill them now. That means you and the army Power Tree are our enemies. When we return, we'll be stronger and harder to take down." Cassie said.

"If you are going to help us then do so otherwise I don't need your threats. So you know I have no family." Luis said.

Cassie smiled at Luis.

"Nor do I. But you still have your uncle and maybe your new girlfriend." Cassie said.

"I'm not dating anyone," Luis said.

"Don't play stupid with me. I know you are dating Lily Griffin. My little sister saw the two of you when you guys returned to school." Cassie said.

"Where is your sister," Lily asked.

"She just died yesterday. Your superhuman father burned her throat." Cassie said in anger.

"I'll be the one killing my father. We are going to sneak behind and attack them." Luis said.

"I understand your hatred for your father. Your plan is good by the way. If you still want an army we should be moving now." Cassie said.

Cassie turned around to face her soldiers. They broke apart to let Luis, Lily, Cassie, and Luis's soldiers pass. After they stood in front the soldiers turned to face Luis. Cassie looked at Luis.

"Lead the way. This is your school after all." Cassie said.

Luis rolled his eyes as he started to jog down the hallway. Dead bodies lay all over the floor headless or missing their throats. He turned a corner then stopped in front of a door. Luis looked at the door then listened quietly.

"What are you waiting for," Cassie asked.

"I'm listening for soldiers," Luis said.

Luis stepped forward. He slowly opened the door. The gunfire continued outside. Something exploded making the dogs bark.

Cassie shushed the dogs then looked back at Luis. He closed the door then turned to Cassie.

"It's just one simple run. We can sprint at them and start killing all of them. Draw your swords and let's get to work." Luis said.

"You heard the man," Cassie said.

After Cassie unsheathed her sword her soldiers followed. Luis kicked open the door then ran outside. He saw Adan and the other captains still fighting. Cassie's dogs jumped at the two soldiers. Luis stabbed a soldier through the back of the head.

"Broken army unsheathe your swords and fight with whatever you have left in you," Luis yelled.

Luke's soldiers started to turn to face Luis. Each step taken forward a body hit the floor. Luke saw Luis chopping off heads and stabbing soldiers. Luis saw his father staring at him. Luke started pushing his own soldiers out of the way. Luis stabbed one last soldier. He blocked an attack from his father.

"How dare you attack your father. I gave your ass life and freedom." Luke said.

"You didn't carry me inside you for nine months. You didn't give me anything, I took my freedom." Luis said.

Luke's hands ignited into flames. He punched Luis in the chest. Luis stabbed his sword into a dead body. Luke watched as Luis took his belt and trench coat off. Luis grabbed his sword and laughed.

"What's so funny," Luke asked.

"Your fire can't harm me or my soldiers in my army. Made some fire proof upgrades." Luis said.

"You don't know my full power. I'm just breaking the surface." Luke said with a laugh.

Luke's entire body ignited into flames. Luis started to dodge swings from Luke. Luis sliced his legs then arms. Luke's blood started to spill onto the floor. He dropped to one knee. Luis went to kick Luke. Luke caught his foot.

"I've finally figured out what the oracle was telling me," Luke said.

Luke spun Luis then got to his feet. Luke tried to kick Luis. Luis regained his balance in time to stab his sword through Luke's leg. Luke screamed in pain as Luis got closer.

"Jackie wasn't a real oracle. She lied to help save those children you had locked away." Luis said.

Luis ripped the sword out of Luke's leg then chopped off his arm. Soldiers from Luis's and Cassie's armies created a circle around Luke and Luis. Luke looked around. Luis dropped his sword as Luke threw a whip of fire around Luis's throat.

"You are the one who is wrong. You are not the dragon. I'm the dragon who saves my Fire Wolves. I'm the one that controls fire and you don't." Luke said with a laugh.

Luke pulled him closer. Luis tried to speak as he put his hands under Luke's chin. Luke loosened the whip a little.

"What did you say," Luke asked.

Luis released the hidden blades. The fire from Luke died. Luis retracted the blades as he started to breathe slowly.

"Not all dragons breathe fire," Luis said.

Luis turned to face Cassie.

"I know I killed Eric but I did it for a good reason." Luis said.

"For you it may have but for me it wasn't." Cassie said with a frown.

"Until we meet again," Luis said.

Cassie and her army turned to leave. Adan and Lily stepped forward.

"What do we do now," Adan asked.

Luis looked in the sky as a military helicopter landed. A tall man with sunglasses stepped out of the helicopter.

"Luis Hernandez and the others in your army I'd like to offer you a job," the man said.

Luis looked at the others. They all nodded at him. He looked back at the military man.

"I'd like you to work for your government. You and your army will be our special forces. We want you to be the ones who go in and kill. This means you do whatever needs to be done to complete your mission." The man said with a smile.

"We'll join under some conditions we have." Luis said.

"What's the conditions," the man asked.

"I want my army's name to stay the same. I also want to be the leader of my army still. I also get to choose what missions we go on. I also want this school bought and built how I want it for our secret headquarters. This secret headquarters will be off all government records so no one can attack us here." Luis said.

"All of your conditions will be met. I'll make sure I see to all of them personally. Now let's get you to your temporary home." The man said.

"We got to make on stop first," Luis said.

The military man nodded as the other helicopters started to land.

The end of part 5

Part 6: Ten Years Later

A woman with cherry red hair and blue eyes stood in front of a dark glass window. A door behind her opened.

"Madam President we have completed the testing," A man said.

"Good, now send them after the hero I have had you look for." The woman said as she turned to face the man.

"Why? He is the most decorated hero we have working for the government." The man said.

"He is a superhuman and we have a new army taking his army's place." The women said with a smile.

"What is this army called," the man asked.

"It's called the Superhuman Hunters," the woman said.

"It will be done Madam President," the man said as he closed the door behind him.

The woman turned to face the window again and smiled.

"Everything you love and have built will be destroyed Luis Hernandez," the woman said to herself.

The End

Printed in the United States
By Bookmasters